"You think I'm some kind of prank. An actress hired to—what? Pretend to have a meeting with you? Then strip out of my clothes?"

He'd started to get a funny feeling. "Well, yeah."

She took a step toward him, and Jet would be lying if he didn't feel as if, somehow, the joke was on him.

"Tell me something, what makes you think the engineer in question is a man?"

"All engineers in the oil industry are men."

She took another step toward him. "There are actually quite a few women in the business. I graduated from Berkley with a degree in geology." She took yet another step closer. "I interned for the USGS out of Menlo Park then moved back to Texas to get my master's in engineering. My father was a wildcatter, and it was from him that I learned the business, so let me reassure you, Mr. Baron, I can tell the difference between an injection hose and a drill pipe. But if you still insist only men can be engineers, perhaps we should call your sister, Lizzie, who hired me."

He couldn't speak for a moment. "Oh, crap."

Her extraordinary blue eyes scanned him, her derision clearly evident. "Still want me to strip?"

He almost said yes, but he could tell that he was in enough trouble as it was.

Dear Reader,

It's always a privilege to be asked to contribute to one of Harlequin's continuity series. When my editor called and explained the premise of the Texas Rodeo Barons, I became even more thrilled. Cowboys, rodeos and family drama? I was *in!*

I will have to admit, it's a little daunting, too. All those different heroes and heroines to keep track of, not to mention story lines and plot twists. I knew I would need to read each book to ensure I didn't drop the ball somewhere along the way.

Those books blew me away.

I was left in awe of my fellow authors: Donna Alward, Trish Milburn, Barbara White Daille, Cathy McDavid and Tanya Michaels. To be honest, I was a little overwhelmed, too. Could I write a book as good as my sister authors? I wasn't sure I could, but I sure tried, focusing all my energy on creating a story that would continue the standard of excellence...and a funny thing happened.

I fell in love with my own characters.

My hero was so much fun to write, and my heroine the perfect match for his bad-boy personality. Add in two adorable twin girls and, well, what a hoot-and-a-half.

I hope you feel the same way about *The Texan's Twins*.

Pamela Britton

THE TEXAN'S TWINS

—

PAMELA BRITTON

⊕ **HARLEQUIN®** AMERICAN ROMANCE®

Special thanks and acknowledgment are given to Pamela Britton
for her contribution to the Texas Rodeo Barons continuity.

Recycling programs
for this product may
not exist in your area.

ISBN-13: 978-0-373-75535-6

THE TEXAN'S TWINS

Printed in U.S.A.

ABOUT THE AUTHOR

With over a million books in print, Pamela Britton likes to call herself the best-known author nobody's ever heard of. Of course, that changed thanks to a certain licensing agreement with that little racing organization known as NASCAR.

But before the glitz and glamour of NASCAR, Pamela wrote books that were frequently voted the best of the best by the *Detroit Free Press,* Barnes & Noble (two years in a row) and *RT Book Reviews*. She's won numerous awards, including a National Readers' Choice Award and a nomination for the Romance Writers of America Golden Heart® Award.

When not writing books, Pamela is a reporter for a local newspaper. She's also a columnist for the *American Quarter Horse Journal*.

Books by Pamela Britton

For the real life twins, Brooke and Gwen.
Two adorable little girls who always amuse and
entertain me. I couldn't have written this book without
you in my life. Know that Auntie Pam loves you.

Chapter One

Hole-lee Toledo—

Jet Baron slammed on the brakes, nearly clocking his chin on the steering wheel in the process.

Dust kicked up from his truck's tires and wafted around the woman's silhouette. A blonde woman—a drop-dead gorgeous woman—in a black dress stared at him curiously as he drifted to a stop.

She waved, mouthed hello, and all Jet could think was, all right, which one of his rodeo friends had set him up? They'd teased him mercilessly last night when he'd told them about the meeting this morning out in the middle of a field in Nowhere, Texas. *Jet Baron, forced to work,* they'd said. Not forced, he'd explained. More like…emotionally blackmailed.

This had to be his friends' idea of a joke because there was no way this was J. C. Marks, their newly hired engineer at Baron Energies. Granted, he'd never met the man, but the point was, J.C. was a man.

"Ha, ha, ha," he said as he slipped out of his truck, the words *Baron Energies* on the side—unlike her truck. "Very funny."

The woman in the black dress stepped away from her vehicle and frowned.

"I beg your pardon?"

Eyes the same piercing blue of an Artic fox scanned first him and then his white truck. She had golden hair, the kind that glowed like pirate's treasure and hung well past her shoulders, and a heart-shaped face complete with a tiny chin and nose. Her huge eyes were outlined with black; it made her appear even more doll-like. This was no engineer with a master's degree in engineering. No way.

"You going to peel off your dress now? Or later?"

"Excuse me?"

"Don't worry. It's not your fault. My friends didn't know I was meeting a man. A project engineer, actually, and you don't exactly look the part. Nice try, though."

Her mouth hung open a bit, and it was a plump, juicy-looking mouth, one that made him think of eating fruit for some strange reason.

"Let me guess. Jet Baron."

"One and the same." He gave her a welcoming smile, his gaze slowly sliding over her body. Damn. Wherever they'd found her, his buddies had outdone themselves. Hot didn't begin to describe her. Damn hot. Holy-moly hot.

"Why am I *not* surprised?" she asked.

Her sarcasm startled him, as did the way she eyed him up and down, her gaze skating over his jeans and black shirt. So direct. So appraising. So…disappointed.

He straightened. "If you're going to start stripping, you better do it now. I'm expecting the engineer at any moment."

She had tipped her head sideways, her long hair falling in large curls over one shoulder. "You think I'm some kind of prank. An actress hired to, what? Pretend to have a meeting with you? Then strip out of my clothes?"

He'd started to get a funny feeling—like he'd walked into a room at the end of a joke. "Well, yeah."

She took a step toward him, and he would be lying if he didn't feel as if, somehow, the joke was on him.

"Tell me something—what makes you think the engineer in question is a man?"

"I was told that."

"By whom?"

He couldn't remember, but it didn't matter.

When his sister had told him to meet with their newest engineer, she'd said Mr. Marks...hadn't she?

"I don't know who told me, just that I know he's a man. All engineers in the oil industry are men, but if you want to pretend you're part of the industry, have at it. Won't matter once you take off your clothes."

She took another step toward him. "Oh, but see? You're wrong." One more step. "There's actually quite a few of us women in the business. I graduated from UC Berkeley with a degree in geology." Another step. "I interned for the USGS out of Menlo Park while getting that degree, then moved back to Texas to get my master's in engineering. My father was a wildcatter, and it was from him that I learned the business, so let me reassure you, Mr. Baron, I can tell the difference between an injection hose and a drill pipe. I've worked on both drilling rigs and production platforms, but if you still insist only men can be engineers, perhaps we should call your sister Lizzie, the one who hired me."

He couldn't speak for a moment, and then all he could utter was "Oh, crap."

Her brows lifted, her extraordinary blue eyes scanning him up and down, her derision clearly evident. "Still want me to strip?"

He almost said yes, but he could tell that he was in enough trouble as it is. "I take it you're J.C.?"

"I am."

Why hadn't Lizzie told him? Then again, why would she? Lizzie had her hands full between helping to run Baron Energies and being newly engaged, not to mention pregnant. The gender of their engineer wasn't exactly something you discussed during the course of a normal conversation, especially when that sister was perturbed with you because you weren't pulling your weight.

"I should apologize."

"You think?"

He almost laughed. "You've got to admit." He pointed a palm toward her dress. "You don't exactly look like an engineer."

She glanced down, then back up. "I have a meeting with our corporate attorney after this. The jacket that goes over this is in the truck, but I don't generally wear one when I'm out of the office and it's nearly ninety degrees outside."

She was right. They were out in a field, on a plot of land his dad had bought years ago and that they'd just recently received the EPA's approval to develop for oil. Nothing but flat pasture as far as the eye could see with a few trees here and there and prickly pear cacti dotting the landscape. He had already begun to sweat, but not because of the heat.

"Okay, I see your point."

"Great, can we get started, then? I have to be in town by five."

Which was probably why she drove her personal vehicle. She was going straight home after her meeting. Damn. Could he have gotten it more wrong?

"Sure, what have you got for me?"

She leaned away from him, her eyes scanning him once again. Whatever she saw must have satisfied her. "Well, as you can see, your dad marked the preliminary drill site."

He glanced at a wooden stick protruding from the ground, one with a neon strip of tape on it and the only indication that something would happen there shortly.

"X marks the spot," he said with a smile.

She ignored his attempt to lighten the mood. "Actually, the presence of reservoir rock affiliated with some uplift erosion there and there—" she pointed toward a slight bulge in the land "—is what marks the spot, but what do I know?"

"I'm guessing a lot more than me," he muttered.

"What was that?"

"Nothing, nothing. Go on."

He might not have spent a whole lot of time working at Baron Energies, but he knew the oil business well enough to recognize an expert, and as she walked him around the job site, pointing toward where they would drill for water and where she thought the reserve pit should go, he admitted she knew her stuff. He'd cut his teeth on rigs, had spent most of his summers working for his dad. When he was fifteen he'd been part of the biggest oil strike on company record. Listening to her speak was oddly...titillating—as if he were in a foreign country and discovered someone who spoke his own language. A sexy someone. Someone with a mouth that drew his attention over and over—

"...questions?"

He realized she waited for him to answer, didn't know what she'd just asked, and so said the first thing that came to mind. "I think we've covered everything." He added a smile.

She stared at him like a teacher who'd caught one of her students with a comic book between the pages of a math textbook. "No, we have not covered everything. I just asked you about the access road."

For the first time in a long, long while he felt his cheeks color. "What about it?"

At some point she must have grabbed a tablet from her truck. Jet didn't remember her doing it. In between watching her mouth and debating with himself on whether or not she had a boyfriend, he'd been a bit... distracted.

"If you're not here to play ball, just go on home." She flipped the cover of her tablet closed. "Go back to rodeo riding or climbing rocks or BASE jumping or dropping out of helicopters or whatever thrill-seeking adventure you have scheduled this weekend. God forbid you should actually work for a living."

So she'd heard about his hobbies. Interesting. Except, he wasn't so sure that was a good thing.

"I work."

"At what?"

"I rodeo full-time."

"That's not a real job."

Actually, it was, but he could tell he'd never make her believe it.

"You're right." He swiped a hand over his hair. "It's not a desk job, and this isn't my usual vocation. At least, it hasn't been for a long while. But with my dad out of commission, I was told I needed to help you manage this project and, believe it or not, I have the experience to do exactly that. It's just gonna take me a while to get up to speed."

"Then maybe you should pay attention."

"I am."

She stared at him as if she could crack his skull open and see inside, and then, finding nothing of interest, shook her own head. "All right, fine. Let's talk about the road." She eyed him skeptically. "Again." She flipped open her tablet once more, sidled up next to him and pointed at the screen. Jet noticed she indicated to a plot map.

Man, she smells nice.

"As you can see, the most direct route would be this way."

Like a flower garden.

"But that would mean building a bridge over the wash."

Was it shampoo? Or perfume? Or maybe body spray.

"As you know, bridges are expensive."

Why hadn't he seen her at the office before?

Because you're never at *the office.*

"It requires engineering and an EIR."

It was true, he rarely made more than an appearance at their downtown office, and it drove his family nuts. His father had never really minded his commitment to rodeo before, but lately he'd been dropping hint after hint that Jet needed to play a bigger part in Baron Energies, especially since Brock's injury. Stupid old fool had climbed on a bull at a seniors' rodeo and damn near broken his neck. Thankfully, it'd just been a broken leg, but he'd been told to stay off his feet and forced to hand over control of Baron Energies to Jet's sister Lizzie. His father had been as subtle as a brick ever since, but his sister's ever increasing girth had sealed the deal. She'd be out on maternity leave soon and his dad had made no bones about Jet stepping in to fill her shoes while she was out of commission. Of course, if Jet had known J.C. was there this whole time, he might have come on board earlier....

"How long have you worked for us?"

She slammed the tablet closed, shook her head in obvious disgust, and said, "I'll have my assistant type up a report and leave it on your desk. I assume you have an office, yes?"

He didn't know. He assumed he did. "Of course." He'd make sure he did.

"Great." She turned away before he could say so much as goodbye.

"Wait!"

She kept walking.

Somehow he managed to catch up and then wedge himself between her and her vehicle. "Look, I really am paying attention."

She released a disdain-filled huff.

"I'm listening to every word. Don't build the bridge. It makes more sense to cut a road coming in from the south. Asphalt is cheaper than steel and an Environmental Impact Report will take months. If it means the laborers will have to drive a few extra minutes to get to the job site, oh, well."

She lifted a brow. A blond brow. Must be her natural hair color, unless she dyed them....

Focus.

"Pretty sure that's what you were going to say, which is why I asked the question. You're good at your job and I'm just a little flabbergasted, is all. You're young, maybe a couple years younger than me, yet you already have a masters? It took me five years to get my bachelor's degree in business management. Of course, I was competing on the PRCA circuit full-time, but still. You must have started college in preschool."

She clutched her tablet as if she wanted to hit him over the head with it. "I was home schooled," she admitted. "I started college when I was sixteen."

Sixteen!

"Did my first two years of college from home through a university extension program. Transferred at eighteen to Berkeley. Graduated when I was twenty with a bachelor's in geology. Spent the next two years working on my masters in engineering. I'm twenty-four and I was hired by Baron Energies right after Lizzie was put in charge, which is probably why I was hired. She understands that a woman can do a man's job."

Yes, his sister did. And J.C. was the same age as him, which made it easier to do the math. "So what have you been doing for the past two years?"

"Excuse me?"

"If it took you two years to get your masters that means you graduated when you were twenty-two. I'm just curious what you've been doing for the past two years."

It was as if he'd turned her into a block of ice, or at least her eyes. "My *point* is, I'm qualified to do the job." And her words were the frosty equivalent of "it's none of your business."

Interesting.

"My sister wouldn't have hired you if you weren't qualified."

"Your sister strikes me as highly intelligent."

Unlike you.

She didn't say the words, but he could have sworn he heard them. It didn't offend him. Not in the least. He liked that she didn't give a fig that he was Jet Baron,

Brock Baron's son, heir apparent to Baron Energies—if his dad had anything to say about it. His last name meant he had his choice of women. And if his last name didn't work, he could usually charm the pants off the opposite sex with a simple smile. Not J. C. Marks.

"What does the *J* stand for, anyway?"

None of your business, her eyes said.

"Just-ina leave me alone?" he quipped.

She stared at him.

"I don't Juan-ita anything to do with you?" he added.

She crossed her arms. She held the tablet in front of her as though it was some kind of shield.

"You're a Jac-queline-ass?"

The arms unfolded.

"Me," he clarified. "I'm the Jac-queline-ass."

"It stands for Jasmine. Jasmine Caroline Marks, and if we're through here, I have an appointment."

He could tell he wasn't getting anywhere—and he kind of liked it. Challenges were what made the world go around, he thought, although he'd never let it get any further than a flirtation. The last thing he needed was his dad breathing down his neck over a sexual harassment lawsuit.

"Sure. Okay. I think we can call it a day."

"Great." She gave him a smile nearly as frosty as a summer soda. "I'll have a cost analysis ready for you in the morning."

"Why don't we meet for breakfast? There's this terrific little coffee shop right down the street from the office."

"I'll see you at the office."

"But the pastries there are terrific. You don't have to eat if you don't want to, though. I'll listen while I chew."

"How does eight-thirty sound?"

"I don't think well on an empty stomach." He really didn't. He was one of those "eats a truckload of food" kind of guys, or so his family claimed.

She headed back to her vehicle. "Then eat before our meeting."

"I'd rather eat with you."

"Not in this lifetime."

"What was that?"

"Nothing," she called, opening the door to her vehicle. He watched her slip inside, grab her cell phone from somewhere, check the display, then tuck it back away.

"See you tomorrow," she said, reaching for her door to slam it closed.

"Looking forward to it."

She started her truck.

"Damn," Jet muttered. Maybe going back to a desk job wouldn't be so bad after all.

Chapter Two

Handsome, arrogant, spoiled son of a gun.

Jet Baron.

Jasmine pointed her truck toward a barely there strip of road, telling herself to forget the man in her rearview mirror.

Why don't we meet for breakfast?

Okay, so she could admit he was beyond gorgeous. And okay, so she hadn't been prepared for the walking mass of masculine virility that was Jet Baron. Seriously. No wonder he'd been voted bachelor of the year two years running by *Dallas* magazine. The man was serious heartthrob material. So what?

You're going to have to work with that walking mass of male virility.

The back end of her truck kicked out. She gasped, then took her foot off the gas. The flat, sun-baked Texas pasture stretched out around her like something from the Old West, nothing but open space for miles, but if she wasn't careful, she might wrap her truck around one of the rare trees that dotted the landscape.

Why did he have to be so good-looking?

And why had everything inside her frozen the moment she'd realized who was behind the wheel? She'd seen pictures of him before. Of course she'd seen them.

Who in the business hadn't heard of Jet Baron? And he'd thought she was a stripper. *A stripper.*

It had taken nearly a year to find a job in the male-dominated industry. A *year.* And in the end it'd been a woman who had hired her. She wasn't going to blow it because, miraculously, there appeared to be one latent hormone floating around her sex-starved body.

Sex starved?

Yes, she admitted to herself, turning onto the main road, a long stretch of blacktop so straight it ended in an arrowhead. It had been years. Unfortunately, Jet Baron stirred urges within her—urges she hadn't felt since becoming a mother to two adorable, wonderful twins. She was a single working mother who didn't have time to eat at a stupid coffee shop, much less get involved with a man.

She was still unsettled the next morning as she walked through the glass entry of Baron Energies. They were on the upper floors of a downtown high-rise. The receptionist, whose name she couldn't remember, smiled as she walked by.

"Good morning," Jasmine said hurriedly.

She'd overslept, not surprising since one of the twins had an earache and the other had decided 1:00 a.m. was the perfect time to start jumping up and down on her bed. Lord, she felt like the walking dead. Somehow she'd gotten Brooke's breakfast smeared on her dress. The oatmeal had left a white stain on the black fabric of her dress that she hoped was covered by her suit jacket, and she had a sinking suspicion that a Cheerio—part of Gwen's breakfast—had fallen down her bra. The moment she passed the reception area she paused, trying to angle her head to see down the swooped neckline.

"Ah, here she is."

The blood drained from Jasmine's face when she looked up. Lizzie Baron. She stood next to the conference room, her dark hair pulled back from her face, a soft blue dress hugging the gentle swell of her pregnant belly. Damn. Just what she needed. The boss.

But she wasn't alone.

Next to her stood a man on crutches and she'd seen enough company literature to know who it was. Double damn.

Brock Baron.

"Dad, this is the new engineer I was telling you about." Elizabeth motioned with her hands, a warm smile on her face, which Jasmine appreciated given that she'd been caught coming in late. "Graduated summa cum laude from Berkeley. Interned at the USGS headquarters. We're real fortunate to have her."

The man who'd founded Baron Energies and built it into a multimillion-dollar corporation might be on crutches, but he was still imposing. Tall and slim, his gray hair was slicked back from his head. He had blue eyes and a gaze that scanned her from head to toe, and not in a good way. She could tell there was something about her appearance that he didn't like. Had he spotted the oatmeal stain?

"This is J. C. Marks?"

And she knew.

Just as Jet Baron had been shocked by her gender yesterday, so, too, was Mr. Baron.

"This is her." She heard the edge of false bravado in Elizabeth's voice.

"Hello, Mr. Baron." She put on her best and biggest smile and moved forward. "I'm so glad to finally meet you. I've heard so much about you from my father that I feel like we've already met."

He adjusted his crutches so he could shake her hand. "Who's your father, honey?"

Honey. In Texas the word was used by men as much as *miss* or *ma'am,* but she had a feeling Brock had used it to make a point to his daughter.

"James 'Mad Hatter' Marks."

She'd used her dad's nickname on purpose, and just as she'd expected, one of Mr. Baron's gray brows shot up. He peered at her intently. "Huh." He seemed to relax a bit. "You look like him."

She turned up the wattage of her smile. "Thank you, sir. My momma always said my daddy was a handsome man."

"Your momma was Caroline Carter, then."

She felt a familiar pang. Her mom had died when she was young, but not a day went by when she didn't think about her or miss her. It was the same way with her dad.

"Yes, sir."

"Good woman, Caroline."

Touched that he remembered her, Jasmine swallowed back the knot of emotion his words had evoked. "Thank you, sir."

"You haven't seen Jet, have you?" Lizzie stepped forward. "We were just in his office and he wasn't there."

Big surprise. She didn't say the words out loud, but she was thinking them. She had a feeling Lizzie was thinking them, too.

"No. I haven't, but we're supposed to meet this morning so I'm sure he's around here somewhere."

Listen to you making excuses for the boss's son. Clearly, you're a sucker for a handsome face.

"I guess we'll keep on looking, then."

But Jet's sister didn't look hopeful. Who could blame her?

The office was a bit of a maze. The conference room to her right overlooked the Dallas skyline. Opposite, in the interior, were offices, including the office of the CEO. One of her coworkers had told her that Brock's office was up front near the reception desk. He liked to eavesdrop on the people who called his company, and he had a habit of going out to the reception area and greeting visitors, even if they weren't there to see him. She suspected he was something of a control freak.

"If you see him, let him know we're looking for him. Come on, Dad. Let's get you back to your office so you can sit back down."

Brock grumbled something about overprotective women, but he nodded at her as he passed. Lizzie Baron stood slightly behind him and so Mr. Baron didn't see the thank-you she silently mouthed in J.C.'s direction, although why Lizzie would thank her she had no idea. She'd been late to work for goodness' sake. She should be *apologizing* to Lizzie.

Her second surprise of the day sat in her office. She drew up short at the sight of a pair of dusty, worn work boots resting on the edge of her desk, a sheaf of papers in his lap, one of them held up in front of him.

"Your dad's looking for you."

The boots slammed down. He about came out of his chair. *"What?"*

"Your dad. He's here. I bumped into him near the conference room."

He leaned back again. "Oh, great."

"You might want to let them know you're here. I have a feeling they both thought you were playing hooky."

"Of course they think that. And just because of that, I think I'll make them wait." He put his boots back up.

"Get your feet off my desk."

Those eyes. Those damn green eyes. They didn't just twinkle, they seemed to...wink at her.

"My, my, my. We're in a bad mood."

Yeah, she sort of was. She hadn't expected to meet the CEO of the company this morning. The man was as sharp as a tack, and while Lizzie didn't seem to mind her being late, she was certain Brock Baron had taken note of it. Plus, she'd been hoping to fish that damn Cheerio out of her bra once in the confines of her office.

"What's the matter? Late night out with the boy-friend?"

She jerked her chair out from beneath her desk, although if she were honest with herself, she was almost relieved to have exchanged her twins for the overgrown child sitting across from her. He was much easier to handle. Despite having Brock Baron as a father, Jet was probably just playing at working until he could get back to his carefree life. Oh, yeah, Lizzie Baron had filled her in on the gritty details yesterday before their meeting. It seemed her brother had been ordered back to work. With Lizzie pregnant, the family hoped Jet would take over her duties. As if that would happen. She would stake her favorite pair of pj's that he wouldn't last two weeks.

"Late night putting together that report I promised you, which I see you received in your email this morning." She tried to pull together the ends of her frazzled nerves. First Brock, now Jet. The bitch of it was, the report she'd put together probably wouldn't even be read by Jet for all that he appeared to be thumbing through it.

"Yeah, thanks." He glanced up and finally let loose the wink she'd seen in his eyes. "Appreciate the hard work. Looks like we're ready to break ground."

Something about that wink made her want to grind her teeth. It was as if he knew how good-looking he was.

As if he thought he could cram pencils up his nose and still charm the pants off her, or the panty hose as the case may be. This morning he wore a white polo shirt with the Baron Energies logo across the left breast. It made his skin, already bronzed by the sun, appear even darker. His green eyes were framed by dark lashes. He looked like his father, she realized, although the eyes were completely different.

"Not until we find a better price on the aggregate." She flipped open her laptop. "I was told the supplier is a friend of your father, but he doesn't seem like a friend to me."

Maybe she should mention her concerns to Mr. Baron himself now that he was in the office. Then again, maybe she should leave well enough alone. More than likely her presence in his office had come as a shock. Well, her female presence. He probably wouldn't welcome hearing her ideas on one of his projects. Not yet, at least. Not until she proved she was every bit as good at her job as a man.

"Yeah, I saw that. Five hundred a load seemed exorbitant."

Her fingers froze on the keys, and she had to work to keep her mouth from dropping open. "I was going to send out an RFP."

"No reason to do that. Let me make a few calls. Pretty sure I can get a better deal."

Clearly, he *had* read the report. "I'm also not very happy with the cost of the drilling crew."

"That I can explain." He set the sheaf of papers down on her desk. Jasmine tried hard to keep from gawking at the new and more serious Jet. "McCoy Drilling is owned by one of my dad's oldest friends. We all know he pads the numbers, but Dad doesn't mind. When my dad was younger, Oscar helped him through some tough times and my dad's been supporting him ever since."

Not only had he read it, he'd absorbed it, too. And he knew something about costing a project if he'd noted where they could cut corners. She leaned back in surprise.

It was like discovering the high heels you'd been wearing all day were dark blue instead of black, and you'd been traipsing around town in a black dress and blue shoes. She couldn't quite reconcile the image of Jet the dilettante with Jet the diligent.

"Yes, well, family friend or no, I would still like to send out a few RFPs to other drilling companies."

"Sure." His smile grew. "Never hurts to try, but my dad can be pretty stubborn."

Based on her initial impression of the man, she wouldn't be surprised. "Duly noted."

His gaze slid past her to the photos on her bookcase, and Jasmine immediately tensed. She tried to move sideways to block his view. Too late.

"Are those your nieces?"

No, no, no. She didn't want to answer questions about Gwen and Brooke. Not today. Not when she was so tired she felt as if she needed to keep her eyes open with Scotch tape and when she was completely off-kilter because of the man sitting across from her.

"Was there anything else you wanted to talk about, Mr. Baron?"

"Are they twins?"

She resisted the urge to rest her head on her arms and groan. Where was a restart button when you needed one?

"I'd like to meet again in a couple days, if you don't

mind. I was hoping to forward our final numbers to your sister by the end of the week."

"Good Lord, are they *yours?*"

"If there's nothing else—"

"They are yours, aren't they?"

He appeared genuinely filled with consternation, and yet also interested in the photo of the girls on Santa's lap. And not the least bit repulsed, which surprised the heck out of her for some reason. She didn't figure him for a family guy.

"Yes, they're twins."

His gaze dropped to her left hand and Jasmine resisted the urge to tuck it in her lap. Too late. He'd spotted the ringless finger, too.

"Divorced?"

"Mr. Baron, as much as I'd like to sit here and chat about my personal life, I have a million things to do today, so if we're through here…"

She stood.

He leaned back and put his boots on her desk again. "Don't get your knickers in a twist."

Her *knickers* in a *what?* "Get your feet off my desk."

"Actually, I think the desk is owned by my family, and I'm just curious. You don't want to talk about your personal life, that's fine, but you may want to sit back down because we have some more things to go over."

What in heaven's name could he have to discuss with her? Plus, she just plain didn't want to sit back down. She wanted to order him from her office, but she couldn't do that. Technically, he was her boss and, technically, as project manager, he might have something to contribute. Goodness, he might actually be doing his job.

"What do you need?"

She thought he might insist on her answering him,

but he seemed to take the hint. "You have an error on page twenty."

She had a— "What?"

"You have 20K on your cost analysis to dig and line the pits, but you put 10K in the projected budget."

She flipped to the page in question, certain he was wrong, but—nope—there it was in black-and-white. She'd grabbed a bad number.

"And then I don't see the costs for cement. You did a cost analysis for the pad, but you didn't pick up that cost in the final budget."

She scanned the page, her cheeks suddenly as flaming hot as a natural-gas flare. She scanned a column and discovered he was right. She'd failed to include the cost for cement. It wasn't a huge expense. Compared to the others, it was a drop in the bucket, but the fact that she'd forgotten...

"Mr. Baron—"

"Jet," he corrected.

"Jet, I don't know what to say. I went over those numbers three times. I was certain I'd grabbed everything, but clearly I didn't."

"Relax. These things happen. That's my job, to look over the engineering costs, combine them with labor and materials and other expenses, and to make sure everyone is on the same page. We'll just change them before we submit the proposal to my sister for final approval and we're good to go."

She shouldn't have been in such a hurry to get him the numbers. She should have just taken her time, sent them to him later, but she was so tired, she honestly didn't know if she'd have caught them later on, either.

"You look exhausted."

Her head snapped up. She tried to control her expression so that he didn't see how close to the mark his words had hit. Didn't work. He tipped his head to the side, and all Jasmine could think was what a waste of a good-looking man. Too bad he couldn't seem to concentrate on any one thing at a time—including his private life based on what she'd heard. Still, someone out there would likely try to snatch him up, if for no other reason than his last name. She, however, would steer clear.

As if he would ever find a single mother of two attractive, she thought. Just the fact that he'd noticed how tired she was said it all.

"Yeah, well, my life is kind of crazy right now."

"All the more reason for you to join me on a little field trip today. Guaranteed to perk you up."

A field trip?

"I can't."

"Sure you can. Since you're new to the company, I thought I'd take you on a tour of our facilities."

She didn't trust the look on his face, nor the gleam in his eyes. "Mr. Baron—"

"Jet," he corrected again.

"Jet," she said with what she hoped was a gracious smile. "I'm really busy today. I'm sorry, but it's just not going to work."

"Sure it is, and since I'm supposed to be taking over as boss, I insist."

She blinked a few times as she tried to gather her thoughts. "And since I'm an employee of Baron Energies, it's my duty to tell you that if you take me away from my desk today, it will put me behind."

"You can catch up later." He stood.

She felt her mouth drop open. The man really didn't know how to take no for an answer. "Your sister asked for my opinion on another upcoming project."

"My sister can wait." He smiled. The man was like a handsome male feline, one with gorgeous black-and-gold coloring and emerald-green eyes and who looked upon the world as if he owned it, tomcat tail straight in the air. "As our newest engineer, you need to familiarize yourself with our assets, unless, of course, you've already had a tour."

She didn't answer.

"Didn't think so." He glanced at his cell phone. "Meet me out in front in an hour. I'll change the numbers and forward this to my sister."

"Wait!" she called as he moved to leave her office. "I can change the numbers."

"No need. I'll do it. It's my job."

"Where did you want to take me?"

He smiled. "I'm a helicopter pilot and twice a year I do an aerial check for HCFs. I'm sure you know the drill."

She did, indeed, know the drill. An aerial survey of hydrocarbon fallout. The EPA mandated such inspections. She was just surprised he was the one that did them. Sure, she'd known he was a pilot, but she assumed that meant he flitted from this rodeo to that.

"How often do you fly?"

The smile grew, catlike green eyes glowing. "Any chance I get." He bounced up on his toes like a teenage boy. "See you in an hour."

And he was gone. She sank down in her chair and covered her face with her hands. Working with Jet Baron wouldn't be easy. Not only did she doubt his commitment to Baron Energies, at least judging by the corporate rumor mill, but there was one other little problem.

She was having a hard time focusing, and not because she was tired, but because his sparkling eyes made her toes curl and because his boyish smile had made her wish, for the briefest of moments, that a man like Jet might find a single mother of twins attractive.

That was the biggest problem of all.

Chapter Three

Jet felt like a kid on Christmas day....

Right up until the moment his dad strolled into the office. Okay, more like hobbled.

"There you are." The tone of his dad's voice was one he recognized from his youth when he'd been off riding one of his horses instead of taking out the trash. "Been looking for you."

Jet leaned back in his chair. The thing about his dad was that you couldn't let him see you sweat. If you did, he'd pounce. "So I heard."

His dad clutched both his crutches in one hand before moving a chair out so he could sit.

"Here." Jet shot up. "Let me help you."

"I don't need your help." Brock gave him what Jet called the Look. He could stop a kid in his tracks with a single glance. "I'm injured, not old."

"No one's calling you old." Jet slowly sank into one of the conference room chairs he'd pilfered last night. He'd discovered he had an office when he'd come back to Baron Energies after his meeting with J.C. Two side chairs and a desk had greeted him. Jet had no idea where the desk chair had gone. He'd wondered if Elizabeth had hidden it on purpose. Probably not, though. She'd turned into a regular professional businesswoman. Frankly he didn't know if he should feel pride or pity. Lizzie had always liked to be in control. The fact that she could do so while winning Daddy's approval was just the icing on the cake, or so he surmised.

"Where were you?"

The third degree. He should have expected that. And he should have expected a visit from his old man this morning, too. Checking up on him. "I was in a meeting."

"With who?" Blue eyes clearly doubted his words.

"With our new engineer." He glanced at his laptop when his email binged. Lizzie. She was warning him their dad was on the prowl. He quickly typed the words *Too late* before turning his attention back to his dad. "We were going over the numbers for the project."

"Oh, yeah?"

Something about the way his dad said the words put Jet on alert. "I was."

Silence. Brock adjusted his crutches again. Jet waited.

"She's good-looking."

Oh, crap. He should have expected this, too. "She's an exceptional engineer."

He didn't know that for sure, not really, but he'd studied the report she'd sent him and from what he could tell, she'd covered all the bases, despite her errors. He could tell he'd surprised her with his knowledge of the industry. The fact was, he'd grown up around wells and drilling. He might not have a masters degree on paper, but he sure as heck did in experience. His father knew that. It was why he was being groomed to take over for Lizzie. The thing was, he liked his life just fine. He helped out at Baron Energies when he could, but this full-time stuff wasn't really his thing.

"She's going to be a distraction to the men on-site."

Jet kept his expression neutral, but he was surprised. For someone who professed to be a man with vision, Brock sure seemed stuck in the past.

"Believe me, she'll keep them at arm's length."

"Sounds like you speak from experience."

Jet glanced at the time. He was supposed to meet J.C. in fifteen minutes but he suspected if he mentioned that to his dad, he'd be treated to another lecture.

"She's a professional, Dad. Even if I was interested in her, which I'm not, she wouldn't give a man like me the time of day."

She'd made her disdain for him obvious. That might have something to do with them getting off on the wrong foot, but that wasn't the only thing he saw in her eyes. She was wary of him. Wary of men in general, and he couldn't help but wonder why.

"Did you know she's the daughter of Jimmy Marks?"

No. He hadn't known that. "She mentioned growing up in the oil fields."

"Best wildcatter I knew. Crazy son of a bitch. Can't believe he had such a pretty daughter. Then again, the girl's mother was a looker."

"She's not my type."

"Just keep your Johnson in your pants."

"Dad!"

"I mean it, Jet. You need to focus. The company needs you now more than ever."

"I'm here, aren't I?"

"Just as long as you stay here."

"Is that it? Is that all you wanted to say to me?"

His dad's eyes narrowed. "No."

Whatever was on his dad's mind, Jet could see it

bothered him. He wondered what it could be. His heart jumped. Was it his health?

"What is it, Dad?"

He saw his dad take a deep breath. "I need your opinion on something."

Well, stop the press. Pigs must surely be flying. Snowballs were being hurled from hell. Rain fell upside down. His dad never asked for his thoughts. Never.

"Your sister Carly came to me a few weeks back asking about your mother."

"Which one?" It wasn't a sarcastic question. Brock had married three times. Once to his birth mom, a woman named Delia, then to Peggy, who'd died when he was fifteen and then to his current wife, Julieta. Frankly, it was Peggy that he mostly thought of as Mom. Julieta was a wonderful woman, but she was more like a friend.

"The one who gave birth to you."

Jet leaned even farther back, placing his hands behind his head as he did so. "What'd she want to know?"

"She's trying to find her."

Jet's hands dropped. "What? Why?"

"I think it has to do with Lizzie being pregnant. Or maybe it's the whole engagement thing. It's got the girls thinking about motherhood and having babies or something. I don't know."

But it bothered his old man, Jet could tell, enough that he was coming to his son and asking for...something.

"What do you want me to do?"

His dad didn't answer for a moment, but what Jet found most telling was the way Brock's gaze never met his own.

"Dad?" he prompted.

"Just keep an eye on the situation for me. See if you can find out what's going on and what they know."

"You want me to spy."

That got his dad's attention. "No. Nothing like that." He reached for his crutches. "I just want to know what they know, that's all."

"Why don't you just ask Carly?"

"Because you know what she's like. Once she gets the bit between her teeth, she's a runaway horse. If she thinks it bothers me that she's looking for Delia, she'll wonder why. That'll get her dander up and, more important, her curiosity rolling. She won't let it rest."

"What's wrong with her being curious?"

Was that a momentary glint of guilt he saw in his dad's eyes? What did the old man have to feel guilty about?

"Nothing wrong with it. I just don't want her getting hurt. That woman did enough damage to our family."

That wasn't it. Jet could tell there was far more to the story than that.

His father stood up. Jet watched, wondered, pondered a bit, but in the end, he admitted now he was curious. "I'll see what I can find out."

"Thank you. I'd appreciate that."

And now gratitude. Would wonders never cease?

His dad put his crutches beneath his arm. "And stay away from that J.C. woman."

"Her name's Jasmine and she's the engineer on the project I'm managing. I can't exactly ignore her."

His dad paused by the door to his office, his reflection projected back to Jet thanks to the glass wall along the front of his office. "You know what I mean."

He did, indeed, know what he meant. Didn't mean he would listen to him, but he knew.

TEN MINUTES LATER, Jet couldn't keep the smile from his face as he exited the elevator amid a crowd of fellow office dwellers. It was a beautiful day in the neighborhood, and if he were honest with himself, he itched to get on a horse.

Those days are over.

No, he silently promised himself. He wasn't going to give up rodeo. And he was getting to do something he loved today. Fly.

But as Jet waited for Jasmine to arrive in front of Baron Energies' corporate offices, he knew he kidded himself. It wasn't just the thought of flying, it was the thought of spending time with Jasmine.

Showing off.

Well, yes, there was that, too.

She was as prickly as a pear cactus, but as his father had noted, as pretty as a Texas bluebonnet, and she sure looked as if she needed a little fun. As it happened, fun was his middle name.

"Let's get this over with."

He hadn't seen her approach. When he turned, he admitted she didn't appear too pleased to be getting away from the office. For half a second he debated whether or not he should let her off the hook. Something stopped him, something that had to do with the exhaustion he saw in her eyes. She struck him as the type who would keep going and going until she dropped, or ended up in the hospital. Twins. That couldn't be easy.

"No need to sound so enthusiastic." He smiled to take the sting out of his words. She'd pulled her hair back in a ponytail. She'd changed, too, though he had no idea where she'd gotten the jeans and white button-down shirt. He wouldn't be human if he didn't admit he liked the dress better, and her long, sexy legs.

"How long is this going to take?" she asked as he held the door of his truck open for her. He'd parked outside their corporate headquarters situated in downtown Dallas and conveniently located just a few blocks from a DART station. They occupied the uppermost floors, and Jet had the oddest sensation of being watched as he stood there.

Dad?

He glanced up, wondering if both Brock and Lizzie stared down at him. He wouldn't be surprised. He'd sent her an email about his outing today, and while it was a task he undertook regularly, the inspection wasn't due for another month. She hadn't replied. Then again, she'd probably been hijacked by their father the moment Brock had left Jet's office.

"Not more than an hour or two. Our holdings aren't that extensive."

He closed the door before she could form some kind of protest or express her displeasure at being taken away from her work. He had to wait a moment for traffic to pass on the busy street in front of their offices. When he pulled open the driver's door a moment later she appeared to be checking messages on her phone. Probably their corporate email.

"Do you ever, I don't know, relax?"

The glare she shot him was like that of an impatient wife, one who'd just been told by her husband to sit down and take a break from chores when she had a million things to do, all of which were being done by *her* and not her husband. He'd seen that look a time or two before on his own stepmother's face when dealing with Brock.

"I have two kids and a full-time job in a demanding field. When, exactly, would I find time to relax?"

He drew back at the sharpness of her tone. She must have seen his reaction because she closed her eyes, sank back against the seat and let out a sigh.

"Sorry," she said softly. "I'm a little sleep deprived. Makes me cranky."

"Me, too."

She opened her eyes again, staring out at the high-rise buildings they passed between, some made of concrete, others made of glass, all of them with people walking out in front. He heard her sigh.

Inside the cab, sunlight flickered through the trees that sprouted up from the sidewalk here and there. The streets were wide, some of the sidewalks made of red brick, but he doubted she noticed such details. Honestly, he would bet what she was really thinking about was a nap.

"Do you have any help at home?"

It was the closest he could come to asking if she was seeing anybody without sounding nosy, or like he was trying to pick her up. Contrary to what his dad might think, he had no intention of getting involved with a woman who had twins. No thanks. Not his cup of tea. Still, he felt sorry for her, watched her closely to see if she would bristle, but she didn't. Instead, she just shook her head, her ponytail shifting over one shoulder and from nowhere came the urge to brush it back, to soothe her brow.

Jet abruptly faced forward.

"I used to have some help."

Her words surprised him because he figured she'd clam up like she always did.

"The twins' grandparents are still alive and they've been a big support, but engineering jobs don't grow on trees and so when I was offered the position at Baron Energies, I took it."

The twins' grandparents, meaning her girls' father's parents. He knew her own dad was dead. Her mother, too. Or so he surmised from the way his dad had made it sound. Did that mean she was all alone? What had happened to the twins' dad?

"I take it the father isn't in the picture."

They were at a stoplight and so he happened to glance at her just in time to see her flinch, almost as if she'd just had a sharp pain, and maybe she had.

"No," was all she said.

Something in her past caused her pain, and he had a feeling it was grief. Sure, he knew some men were irresponsible jerks and that it was completely plausible that she'd been ditched by the father of her twins, but he didn't think so. There'd been something in her eyes, her remarkable eyes, that he suddenly realized were tinged by a perpetual sadness.

"So who watches your twins when you're at work?"

She seemed to snap out of a momentary trance. He noticed how long her lashes were when she blinked.

"I hired someone. A woman in my condominium complex. She was looking to make some extra money and I didn't want to be shuffling my girls between their home and a day-care center. She comes to my place every morning."

"I bet you wish she would come in the middle of the night sometimes, too."

She glanced at him in surprise, but then something remarkable happened, something that left him feeling as if he'd been kicked in the gut.

She smiled.

"You have *no* idea."

Chapter Four

She'd revealed too much, Jasmine thought a few minutes later. She should have kept things impersonal. Chatted about Baron Energies' last quarterly report or something. Instead, she'd treated him like a Catholic priest, someone to confess all her dirty little secrets to, and that was the stupidest thing in the world to do. He was the boss's son. A man who reported back to the big man himself, not to mention his sister. The last thing she needed was for word to get out that she was stretched too thin, that she couldn't cope, that she'd made mistakes.

"Ever been up in a helicopter before?"

Her stomach dropped.

"No."

To be honest, she hadn't given the coming ride much thought other than how much it would interfere with her day.

"You want the vanilla ride, then? Or the Disneyland version?"

"Explain Disneyland version?"

He smiled, and Jasmine thought he looked like a kid standing in front of an amusement park. This was the second time she'd seen him with mussed hair. He trimmed the black strands shorter on the sides than on the top and it appeared he frequently ran his fingers through it. If it weren't for the strong jaw and the curve of his masculine lips, she'd think him younger than her, and those green eyes had laugh lines stretching out from the corner. He was tan and well-groomed and so good-looking there was no way he didn't know the effect he had on women.

Like you?

No, she told herself firmly. *Not like me.*

"Well, we could fly straight to our destination, or we could take the scenic route."

"Why do I have the feeling the scenic route entails a lot more ups and downs?"

The lines stretching from the corners of his eyes deepened as he smiled. "Because you'd be right."

"I see."

"You don't get airsick, do you?"

This was beginning to sound more and more ominous. "No."

"You like scary rides?"

Yes. A long time ago. She'd lived life on the edge. You didn't date a hellcat without having a wild streak of your own. Alas, motherhood and loss had cured her of that.

His face fell. "I can see by your face that you'd like me to take it easy."

"No." The word shot out of her before she could stop it. Something in his eyes had challenged her, and that should scare the crap out of her. Darren had challenged her, too, and look where that had gotten her.

"No?" he asked, as if sensing her doubts.

"I don't mind a little excitement."

She shouldn't have said the words. The way he glanced at her, quickly, that wink back in his eyes.

"Oh, really?"

She blushed. "I meant I'm not as uptight as I look." This was going from bad to worse, so she did the only thing she could think of. She changed the subject. "What did your dad want?"

As a buzzkill, the words worked perfectly. He frowned, and somehow she knew what he was thinking. "He was checking up on me."

"You mean, making sure you were at work."

He glanced at her quickly. "Something like that."

"You're not very happy about being forced into a day job, are you?"

"Excuse me?"

Don't look at him. Easier to focus that way. "Your... lack of interest in Baron Energies is well-known."

"See, that's where everyone's wrong." He smoothly merged onto I-35. "It's not that I'm not interested. I love our family business. I just don't see the point of devoting my entire life to it like my dad, at least not while I'm young. I have my whole life to do that."

Must be nice to have that kind of attitude. She'd had to work her entire life to get to where she was. As a woman she'd had to do things better, be smarter, work harder. Lizzie Baron had been the first oil executive to take her seriously and yet here she was with her brother, a man who didn't want what had been handed to him on a silver platter, and she couldn't help but feel a small burn of resentment. What would it be like to never have to worry? To have such a huge support group that you knew you'd always be taken care of? She'd left behind her only support, Darren's parents, and they were aging help at that. Even so, she would miss them—*did* miss them—terribly. They were the only family she had.

"I don't have my whole life ahead of me," she heard herself say. "I only have the here and the now."

Only after she said the words did she wonder why in the name of heaven she'd made the confession. That's what happened when the only company you kept were twin girls. Girlfriends? What were those? Any fledgling friendships she might have formed once she'd graduated college were toast now that she'd moved. As she sat there thinking about it, she admitted she'd never felt more alone in her life than in that moment sitting there with *Dallas* magazine's bachelor of the year next to her.

He stared at her, she realized. Analyzed her. Tried to determine the look on her face.

Unhinged mother.

She wanted to tell him that's what he saw. Someone living life on the edge…and about to come unglued.

"You okay?"

No. She was most definitely not okay because following on the tail of her loneliness came an unbidden urge to cry. It made her angry, that urge. She'd never been one for stints of self-pity, yet here she was, suddenly looking out the side window of his sixty-thousand-dollar truck and wondering if she had the strength of will to hold on to her tears.

"Fine." But even to her own ears her voice sounded high, her nose clearly stuffed with the crud that clogged your nostrils and your throat when you tried so hard not to weep.

He flicked on his directional. It took her a moment to recognize the *click-click* of his blinkers, and then a moment more before she realized what he was about to do.

"No," she said. "No, no, no. Do *not* pull over. I'm fine."

"You need a tissue."

"I do not."

But, damn it, she *was* crying. *Crying.* In front of Jet Baron.

He pulled over.

When she glanced through her lashes the world was a blurry mess. She had no idea where they were and so she sucked in a breath, hoping it would help to clear her eyes and her airway, which made her sound like an asthmatic yappy dog, and that only made her want to cry even more.

"You've had a rough spell, haven't you?"

It was too much. The long night. The early morning. The mistakes on her report. Meeting Brock Baron. Seeing the surprise in his eyes. No. It went back further than that. Losing Darren. The new job. The move away from everything she loved.

"I really don't want to talk about it."

A blurry box formed in front of her eyes. Tissue. She had no idea where he'd pulled it from. Reluctantly, she snatched one and dabbed at her eyes. At least the urge to sob seemed to have faded. Could she be hormonal? Was it close to her time of month? To be honest, she couldn't recall anything. Time seemed to be an endless blur of get up, take care of the twins, get ready for work, race around the office, go home, cook dinner, bathe the twins, tuck them into bed, fall into her own bed—exhausted—then get up and do it all over again.

"You mind me asking why the father of your twins isn't doing more?"

Another sucked-in breath, this one hitching in her chest again. "Oh, you know," she said airily, waving her hand through the air. "He's a little busy, what with being dead and all."

Silence.

From the left side of the vehicle came the *whoosh* of

a car passing them. He'd pulled to a stop at the base of an off-ramp—she had no idea where. To their left cars whizzed by on the freeway. Actually, she was kind of glad she'd stunned him into silence. It gave her a moment to catch her breath.

"Wow," he said at last. "You've been handed a rotten deck of cards, haven't you?"

He had that right.

"When? How?"

She stiffened.

"If you don't mind me asking."

He handed her another tissue. This time she took it without hesitating. She'd stained the first one black. Great. She probably looked like a panda bear.

"He was a hellfighter."

And that said it all. Jet Baron was no fool. He knew what a hellfighter did. Knew the risk involved in trying to put out the flames of a burning oil well. She'd known, too. She'd warned herself away from Darren at least a half a dozen times that first night they'd met, but something about his bright blue eyes and his sparkling smile and the way he'd stared out at the world—as if he'd owned it and so nothing bad would ever happen to him—had drawn her to him like a kitten to catnip. She'd thought him invincible. She'd been dead wrong.

"So I take it he died on the job?"

"Yup. Two months before we were supposed to get married. I found out I was pregnant afterward. Darren never even knew."

"Damn." He shook his head. "That's a tough gig."

"Eyup."

She felt better now. At least her lungs didn't sound like a clogged exhaust pipe. Just a momentary breakdown. No big deal.

Except you broke down in front of the boss's son.
Who's staring at you right now.

She had to look away again. What she needed was a swift kick in the rear. That's what Darren would have done. He'd never let her wallow in self-pity.

"Do you need anything?" Jet asked. "A helping hand? A shoulder to cry on? A shot of whiskey?"

That actually made her smile. "No." She leaned her head against the smooth leather seat. No faux leather for the prince. "I'm fine."

He stared at her again, and she wondered what he saw. A woman with raccoon eyes and tear-stained clothing, no doubt. She glanced down and realized she did indeed have a Cheerios in the cup of her bra. She should have known.

"How long has he been gone?"

Damn it, why *shouldn't* she feel sorry for herself? It sucked big-time that she had no one to count on, no husband to help ease her burden, no family to share in the raising of her children. And her girls…her poor girls. They would never know their father. That, more than anything, broke her heart.

"Jasmine?"

"Five years ago."

She wasn't looking at him, but she could tell her words surprised him.

She inhaled, released her breath, inhaled again. She did that over and over again until her eyes stopped burning and her heart stopped breaking—but the cracks would always remain.

"You've been doing this a long time on your own."

Yup. School. Working whatever job she could find. Raising the girls.

"I'm sorry," he added. "Nobody should ever have to raise a child on their own, much less two."

Damn it, she felt her eyes begin to burn again. She didn't want him to see her like this. Didn't want him to be nice to her. She wanted to go back to the way things had been this morning when she'd walked into her office and she'd been looking down her nose at him. Jet Baron the dilettante. Instead, he'd fixed her report, invited her to tour his family's facilities and handed her tissue.

"I am, too," she said.

She heard him shift. A hand reached for her own. She thought about twisting in her seat, turning away so he couldn't do what he was about to do—touch her. Instead, she watched as long fingers enveloped her own. Warm fingers. Soft fingers. No. Not soft, she realized. He had calluses on the inside. He worked outdoors a lot, she remembered. Rodeo.

"Let's see if we can't put a smile back on that face of yours."

He released her.

Jasmine couldn't move. It had been a long time since a man had touched her. A long time since she'd felt soft tingles of desire skate up and down her arm. A long time since she'd experienced the need, the want, the longing to have a man do more than touch her.

Dear God.

She was attracted to Jet Baron.

Chapter Five

They arrived at the community airport less than fifteen minutes later, although Jet kept sneaking glances at his passenger the whole time. She'd spent the first five minutes fixing her makeup, not that she needed any, he thought. She was quiet now, which, he supposed, was better than crying. He hated when women cried—and with three older sisters, he'd seen a lot of crying over the years.

"You know, Baron Energies sponsors the Mid-Texas High School Rodeo Association."

She shot him a look that clearly asked, "Yeah, so?"

He turned into a side entrance to the airport. Off-white metal buildings were directly ahead, many of them housing airplanes and aviation mechanics. The helicopter they leased was at the end of the block, so to speak, where Jet turned right and followed a road that skirted the main runway. He pulled into a spot marked for Air Dynamics customers.

"Anyway," he said, putting the car in Park and shutting off the engine. "This weekend is their annual fundraising rodeo."

When he glanced at her it was in time to spot the "Where is this going?" look in her eyes.

"It's fun. You should bring your girls."

The "where is this going?" faded into "are you out of your mind?"

"A lot of employees take their families. There's pony rides and games for the kids and lots of fun stuff to do. My brothers and I give a clinic." At her look of confusion, he added, "We work with some of the high schoolers on their rodeo skills. My sister can give you more information and tickets, too, if you're interested."

He knew she was going to say she was too busy. Or that it'd be too difficult to manage her girls on her own. Or that she had work to do...*something,* but he didn't give her time to respond.

"Come on." He opened his door. "Let's get going."

He assumed she'd follow, and she did. Hot, humid air instantly clung to the white polo shirt he wore. As he walked toward the leasing office that handled the maintenance and upkeep of the helicopter he flew, he didn't glance back, just held the glass door open for her when the time came, cool air blasting the both of them.

"Mr. Baron," said the owner of the company with a wide smile. The man had taught him how to fly, and so Jet smiled back. "I was wondering if you'd changed your mind about flying today."

"Sorry, Eric. We were a little delayed."

The man glanced at Jasmine, and Jet spotted the telltale interest that sprang into his eyes. Who could blame him? Despite the tears she'd shed earlier, those gorgeous blue eyes of hers were as big and as lovely as ever. Her hair might be drawn back in a ponytail, but it flattered a face that didn't need makeup to look beautiful. As Jet watched a welcoming smile form on Eric's face, he felt his own smile fade, something that alarmed him slightly. There was no way he'd ever ask a woman like her out. He preferred females that weren't looking for a commitment and there were plenty on the rodeo circuit. Sure, a few of them might want more, but he'd gotten adept at avoiding the parson's noose. Women like Jasmine—someone with two kids to complicate things even further—were to be avoided at all costs.

"This is J. C. Marks, our new engineer."

"Afternoon, Ms. Marks," Eric said, and if he'd been wearing a hat, Jet was certain he'd have tipped the brim.

"Thought I'd give her a tour of our holdings while I check the lines."

"Lucky you," Eric said, but Jet wasn't certain if he meant lucky for Jasmine to get a helicopter ride, or lucky him for getting to ferry around such a good-looking passenger. He suspected the latter, especially since the man couldn't keep his eyes off Jasmine as Jet filled out paperwork.

"We've already done the preflight." Eric checked his watch. "We'll see you back here in two hours."

Jet motioned for Jasmine to follow.

"Why do I have a feeling this is less about work and more about having fun?" she asked.

"Because it is going to be fun." He glanced back at her. "Something tells me you need a little of that."

"Please." And the way she said it reminded him of yesterday. "You make me sound like a charity case."

"You were just crying in my truck. I wouldn't be human if I didn't want to cheer you up a little." He headed toward the gleaming black helicopter parked in a painted white circle. "All you have to do is hang on and enjoy the view."

Her steps slowed as they approached the piece of equipment. He tried to see things through her eyes. It was a midsize helicopter. Not huge, but not a crop duster, either. The nose had been fitted with a "sniffer" a special device that would detect HCF emissions. This was a portable version that AirDyn—as they were called for short—could take on and off as needed. Inside the cockpit a laptop would record their findings, although Jet really didn't expect any blips on the monitor. Baron Energies spent a small fortune ensuring the safety of their wells.

He opened the door. She didn't move. He turned to her in surprise.

She kept glancing from him to the helicopter and then back again, like a kitten fascinated by a moth. "You mind me asking how long you've had your pilot's license?"

"About a month."

Her gaze froze.

"Kidding, kidding." He lifted his palms. "I've been flying for years. Been piloting helicopters for just as long. Makes things easier when you're hitting up a bunch of rodeos and it's convenient for my dad when he gets the urge to go out and check the wells, which he likes to do pretty frequently. Control freak with a capital *C* and *F*."

She glanced at the helicopter again. He knew what she was thinking.

"Really," he said. "It's okay."

He could tell she didn't want to admit her fears. To her credit he saw her take a deep breath, square her shoulders and step forward.

Good girl.

"There's a headset between your seat and mine." She looked around once she'd settled herself. He could tell she instantly spotted the headset. "Make sure you strap yourself in. It can get a little rough sometimes. Downdrafts and all that. I'm going to walk the exterior."

She still looked green around the gills, but she would change her mind once they were airborne. It was amazing up there, and she wanted a little excitement. He couldn't wait to give it to her, although he worried about why he needed to please her. The familiar pre-flight quickly garnered all his attention, however. As he walked the aircraft, his heart began to pound. Flying was one of the few things aside from riding a bull that gave him an adrenaline rush.

He climbed inside a moment later, glancing over at Jasmine as he did so. She'd put on her headphones in a way that flattened her hair against her scalp, a big loop of her ponytail stuck inside the earpiece, but it didn't detract from her pretty face. Quite the contrary. It highlighted the perfect shape of her cheekbones and her large blue eyes.

"Ready?"

"No."

He bit back a smile. "Relax. Flying is the *other* thing I do really well."

He didn't mean for the words to sound so flirtatious, but she clearly took them the wrong way, judging by the look she shot him. "I'll try and remember that if we start to crash."

He donned his headphones. "Can you hear me?"

"Yes," she answered back, her voice sounding tinny and far away. "But that might not be a good thing when I start screaming."

"That's okay. I have a mute button."

He flipped a switch, and the rotors began to spin, slowly at first and then faster and faster. What started as a minor vibration turned into a major one and then slowly smoothed out until there was nothing but the near-deafening hum of the engines. He touched the comm, checked in with the tower, received clearance to fly in a northwesterly direction. Didn't matter how many times he flew, there was always the surge of adrenaline just before he set off.

"You ready?"

"No."

"Here we go."

SHE WANTED TO PUKE.

Honestly, when he'd dragged her along, she hadn't given a thought to Jet actually piloting the craft. Well, maybe she'd thought about it a little bit, but now that moment of truth had arrived.

"Please don't kill me." The words just sort of popped out. "I have two little girls who really need their mother."

They were slowly rising above the earth, the metal building they'd just been inside shrinking like a piece of plastic in the oven.

"Hey, relax."

"I just don't think it was very smart of me to trust a man who's known for never following through on much of anything in life."

"Excuse me?"

It helped to take her mind off things to keep talking, even if she was pretty sure he might not like what he was about to hear. "There was the race-car thing."

He turned the nose of the helicopter. They shot forward. She reached for a bar on the door, but there was no bar on the door. This wasn't a car. This was a helicopter and apparently there was no need for something to hang on to according to the manufacturers.

"The car-racing thing was a dare. Someone claimed he had a faster car than mine. I proved him wrong."

"By building your own drag car."

"It was a stock car, way different than the big-ended, fat-tired things you see on TV."

"And then there was the stint as a writer."

"Where did you hear about that?"

They were at least a mile above the airport, cars shrinking to the size of pill bugs, highways looking like the veins of a leaf spreading in all directions, and buildings resembling Lego blocks. Off in the periphery, the greens and golds and sometimes the blue of rural Dallas County stretched as far as the eye could see.

"The energy business is a small world. People talk."

They were picking up speed—Jasmine reminded herself that she'd asked for a little excitement. Still, it was one thing to ask, another to experience his version of excitement firsthand.

"First of all, it was cowboy poetry, which isn't the same thing as trying to be a writer, and I was actually pretty good at it."

You haven't flown since before having Brooke and Gwen.

Was that it? Was she suddenly aware of her own mortality now that she'd given birth?

Keep talking.

"Okay, and how about trophy fishing?"

"*That* I still like to do."

"My point being you never seem to settle down and do one thing at a time." She swallowed back her agitation. "Which means you're never going to excel at anything you do."

"Ouch."

"Except rodeo. You seem to have stuck with that."

"And to think, I actually felt sorry for you a little while ago."

"I'm just worried your lack of commitment might mean you're not the best helicopter pilot in the world."

"That worry I can dispel right now."

"Oh, yeah? How?"

"Remember when I asked you if you wanted the Disney or the vanilla version?"

"Yeah?"

"Here's the Disney."

"Oh, damn—"

Her stomach lurched. It actually felt as if it flew out of her body and landed somewhere in the vicinity of her toes. In reality, it was the helicopter that dropped, but it might as well have been her stomach. She screamed, or she thought she did. Her terror might have been solely confined to the inside of her head.

"Hang on."

She almost yelled there was nothing to hang on *to,* but she was too busy trying to catch her breath. They were headed for a patch of green, one with a ribbon of blue in the center of it. A river. She had no idea which one it was, only that they were headed right for it, the helicopter dropping lower and lower and lower.

"Jet!" But it wasn't exactly a squeal of terror. Even to her own ears she could hear the laughter.

They never even got close to the water, not really, but it felt like it as Jet maneuvered the helicopter forward. Below she caught a glimpse of two startled fishermen.

"Bet you've never seen the Trinity like this."

No. She hadn't. Now that she could breathe again she'd begun to notice things. They followed the path of the river, skating over the treetops like a dragonfly, the aircraft gently swaying left and right.

And it was beautiful.

Away from downtown the river glowed like a ribbon

of mercury. She spotted more watercraft and nearby homes and even the occasional flock of birds, their reflections sliding across the water's surface.

"Hang on," he said again.

This time he didn't jerk the wheel or the paddle or whatever it was called. He smoothly turned left. They crossed over the top of a thick grove of trees, over a batch of industrial buildings, the shadow of the helicopter growing bigger and then smaller as they flew over the tops of trees and buildings. They seemed to burst into a clearing. A pasture of some kind. Cattle jerked their heads up as they flew overhead, gone in the blink of an eye. Jet dropped the craft lower and then lower still.

"Aren't you, I don't know, worried about power lines or something?"

"Nope." He peered ahead, a look of concentration on his face as he worked the controls. "Done this a thousand times."

"Or small planes?"

"They're not allowed below a thousand feet. Helicopters can go wherever they want below a thousand without tower approval."

"So if we crash, no one will know where we are?"

"They'd find us with our transponders."

She digested that bit of information. "So what you're telling me is you can go anywhere you want without anyone telling you no."

"Pretty much, but we can't fly over airports. And if we headed toward an army base we might get shot down."

"Then do me a favor. Steer clear of the military."

"Will do."

She'd started to relax. They were like Pegasus galloping through the sky, low enough that she could make out thick patches of prairie grass, but not so low they were in danger of hitting something. He angled the craft to the right, a grove of trees getting closer and closer, her body tensing and then—*whoosh*—up they went, over the tops, back down into the river basin and she was smiling and, yes, giggling.

"There it is," she heard him say. "I knew it was in there somewhere."

"What?"

"Your laughter."

She glanced over at him. He did the same, just a quick look because he was busy piloting the craft, but what she saw in his green eyes made her smile fade. Pleasure. Warmth. Satisfaction.

"You should laugh more often."

He'd looked away again, but she couldn't stop staring at him for some reason. She told herself to turn away, but she couldn't because she'd been dumbfounded by a sudden realization.

Jet Baron was a really nice man.

And she liked him.

Chapter Six

Sooner or later they had to get down to business, although Jet was sorry when it came time to check the transmission lines. He showed Jasmine the transfer station where all of Baron Energies' oil and gas lines terminated. From there it was a simple process to follow them out to the individual wells. He hadn't been kidding when he suggested the trip was a good way for her to become familiar with their holdings. Seeing the individual wells up close—well, from a few hundred yards overhead—gave her a better picture of the kind of work they did. Plus, it afforded him the opportunity to give her the history of each well.

"I'm impressed," she said two hours later. "I had no idea you knew so much about your family's holdings."

He had to call into his local tower advising their return before answering, "Why wouldn't I know about them?"

She shrugged a little. "I guess I thought your main focus these days was the rodeo."

"Actually, it might surprise you to know that I've been working for my dad on and off for years. I even managed to get a degree in business management while off doing those rodeos."

He'd actually surprised himself when he'd earned that

degree, he admitted to himself as he brought the helicopter in for a landing. He hadn't exactly been trying. Going to college was just something he did in between following the rodeo trail. It wasn't as though he'd ever wanted to run Baron Energies. That was his dad's dream, not his own, and if he were honest, Lizzie would be better at it. Once he'd realized his sister was pregnant, however, he'd been feeling the pressure. It didn't help that Lizzie refused to slow down. She'd had a health scare early in her pregnancy and it'd been that more than anything that'd convinced him to step up to the plate. He'd never forgive himself if something happened to his big sis. So here it was. Sooner or later he'd need to pick up the slack, especially since his dad seemed content to sit back and let him do exactly that. That was his evil plan, Jet figured, only suddenly he didn't mind so much.

"There you go." He cut the engines once the skids were firmly on the ground. "Back safe and sound."

The rotors still spun, but their loops became lazier and lazier with each passing second. The sound quieted, too. Jet took off his headphones. Jasmine did the same.

"Thanks for the tour."

He scanned the gauges one last time before killing the power. "I told you it'd be fun."

She looked as though she didn't want to smile, as if she fought the urge to admit that she'd enjoyed herself. "It was a nice change of pace."

If that's all she'd admit, he'd take it.

"Come on. I'd better get you back to the office before my sister issues an APB."

It was worse than that. When he got back to their headquarters none other than Lizzie herself sat in his office chair, hands resting on a belly that seemed to have sprung a huge bulge overnight, dark hair pulled back from her face, eyes full of censure.

"Have fun?" she asked.

Why did he always feel like a kid caught in a pen of bulls around his sister? "I did, thanks," he said with his best love-me-because-I'm-so-cute smile.

Didn't work.

"J. C. Marks is off-limits."

Since his sister didn't appear to want to move, Jet took the seat his dad had sat in earlier. "So dad tried to warn me this morning."

Her eyes flashed, although not because of him, Jet could tell. She was thinking about their dad's visit to the offices—and not in a good way.

"That man will be the death of me."

"Was he the one that told you to warn me off Jasmine."

"Jasmine, is it?"

He felt his cheeks tingle. Damn it. That only ever happened when he was around Lizzie. She'd taken on the role of mother when his real mother had left and so sometimes it felt as if she really were his mom. There were seven years between them, but sometimes the age gap seemed like a lifetime.

"And as it happens," she said, "Dad didn't say a word about Ms. Marks."

"I'm surprised he let you hire her."

Lizzie's eyes darted away for a moment and he knew his earlier guess had been right. "He didn't know about her, did he? You hired her without him knowing *she* was a *she*."

"I don't answer to Dad, not while I'm in charge, and you're not going to change the subject. *Jasmine* is off-limits."

"You know, I've never understood the term *off-limits*. A limit of what? Land? Sea? Air? If it was land, wouldn't it be she's out of the limit? Not she's off-limits?"

"Jet."

"Yes?"

"Shut up."

He sank back in his chair, mimicked her pose, making sure to shove his belly out ever so slightly just so she knew he was mimicking her ever-increasing girth.

Her eyes narrowed. "It took me months to find J.C. Months. And I didn't hire her because she was a woman. Frankly, I was surprised a candidate with her credentials hadn't already been snapped up by one of the big energy companies like BP or Shell. That she ended up here right when I needed her most is a small miracle and you will not mess this up with your philandering ways."

"You make it sound like I have a habit of cruising the halls of Baron Energies for hot chicks."

She leaned forward. "Are you kidding? We've been lucky in the past to see you in the halls at all. Now here you are, finally ready to work a forty-hour week, and right away you're off with our new engineer."

"Did you know she has twins?"

"Yes."

"And that the father is dead."

She drew up sharply. "I figured he was out of the picture, but I didn't know he was dead."

"He died before they were born. The man was a hell-fighter, Lizzie. He never even knew she was pregnant."

"I didn't know that." Her eyes suddenly narrowed. "Wait. How did you find that out?"

He thumbed his hand toward outside. "She had a total breakdown on the way to the airport. To be honest, I think she's a little sleep deprived. She looked like death warmed over when she got in this morning. That's why I invited her to tag along. She looked like she could use a break."

"I saw her this morning, too."

"Then you know what I'm talking about."

"She was late."

"She was tired."

Long stare. "She still made a good impression on dad."

"I'm not surprised."

For a moment he was tempted to change the subject by asking Lizzie what she knew about Crazy Carly's latest ploy to find their birth mother, but his dad hadn't mentioned anything about Lizzie knowing. Maybe he should wait until he talked to Carly.

"Define breakdown."

Uh-oh. He didn't want to get Jasmine in trouble, either. "It was no big deal. She just opened up about some things. I think she was feeling overwhelmed." Lizzie's eyes narrowed even more. "Not because of work. Because of the twins."

Silence. Jet feared he'd said too much, but his sister's gaze caught on a sheaf of paper resting on his desk. "Well, if she's overwhelmed, you wouldn't know it. The report she put together looks great."

He wanted, oh, how he wanted, to tell his sister that he'd been the one to catch Jasmine's errors, but discretion was the greater part of valor and so he held his tongue.

"Yeah, she's doing great so far."

His sister snorted as if to say he was hardly in a position to judge, and to be honest, it kind of got his dander up. "Hey, I contributed to that report, too."

"Yeah." Small smile. "I'm sure you did."

"I did."

Her smile grew. "My point being that you're here to do a job, not make nice to our newest employee."

"I invited her to the benefit rodeo this weekend."

Her eyes widened. "Invited her as in a date?"

"No, no. Of course not."

She let out a loud breath.

"Look, Lizzie. Jasmine's not my type, okay? I don't know what everyone's all worried about."

"She's gorgeous."

"She's the single mother of twins. When have I ever dated a woman with kids before?"

His words had the desired effect. He watched his sister's shoulders relax.

"I thought it'd be a fun event for her twins, that's all."

Lizzie nodded. "If she mentions it, I'll give her tickets."

"I thought I'd drop them by her office."

The death stare returned. "Jet, I'm sure I don't have to explain the consequences of even the most innocent of flirtations. You say you're not interested in her, not in that way, but you have a habit of charming the pants off a woman without her even realizing it until it's too late. She might think you're serious or something and file a sexual harassment suit."

He shot up in his seat. "Sexual—" He couldn't speak for a moment. "I'm not going to sexually harass her."

"I know that and you know that, but you can't be holding her hand just the same."

"I didn't hold her hand." Okay, so maybe he had, but Lizzie didn't need to know that. "I offered a tissue."

"She was crying?"

Crap. This was going from bad to worse. The last

thing Jasmine needed was for Lizzie to think her unprofessional because of something he said.

"Look, she came in this morning looking like death warmed over. When I learned she was a single mom, raising twins, I thought I should be nice to her. I don't think it's a stretch to say it's been a long time since someone's showed her kindness. She's in a new city, on her own, no help from the twins' grandparents, and I felt bad for her. I don't think I need to explain to you what it'd be like to raise not one, but two kids all by yourself."

His sister had the grace to blush. Everyone knew Lizzie had been knocked up by her new fiancé. He'd even heard a thing or two about a certain night at a certain rodeo when his sister had been seen leaving a bar in Fort Worth with Chris Miller. Bah-dah-bing, bah-dah-boom, they're suddenly engaged. His whole family had done the math. That was six months ago and Lizzie was exactly six months pregnant.

Hello.

"I feel sorry for her," he said.

And you think she's hot. Okay, so he did, but it wasn't going anywhere.

"I thought maybe she'd like to do something fun with her twins, something that would give her a sense of family."

He'd struck a nerve. His sister had lost all her bluster. She almost seemed to be lost in her own little world for a moment.

"Okay, fine. I'll do my best to ensure she attends this weekend's festivities. Tell her we expect her to support the cause."

"'Atta girl."

A finger wagged in his direction. "But I expect you to keep your distance, Jet. Don't go all knight in shining armor on me. I don't want her getting the wrong impression. I really like this woman, even more so now that I know what she's been through. Keep your distance."

He gave his sister a Roman salute, pressing his fist against his heart. "As you wish, my liege."

His sister frowned.

He gave her his most charming smile. His sister had nothing to worry about. Jasmine Marks might be hot, but he wasn't into baby mamas. No way. Too many complications.

Strange how much he was looking forward to meeting her twins, though. Strange and kind of alarming.

HELICOPTER RIDES, FANCY trucks and an invite to a rodeo this weekend. All in all, it'd been a day Jasmine wouldn't soon forget.

"Mom-ma!" Gwen cried, the four-year-old charging away from Mrs. Dalton, the woman Jasmine had hired to watch her kids during the day, and heading toward her at a speed that Jasmine didn't like. She held her breath as Gwen ran between the kitchen table and a stainless-steel garbage can.

"Hey, baby." She held out her arms and then lifted Gwen into her arms. "How was your day?"

"Good," she said, her pudgy little fingers swiping a lock of hair off Jasmine's face, the gesture so motherly Jasmine felt her throat clog for the second time that day. What would she do without her baby girls?

"Good evening, Ms. Marks."

The woman was a godsend. A grandmother to two little girls of her own she'd quickly won the girls over. She resembled Darren's mother, too, with her bushy gray hair and wide smile and her penchant for wearing bright colors. Jasmine counted her blessing to have met her the day she'd moved into the complex where she lived.

"We just had dinner. Brooke insisted on playing with her model horse afterward."

Brooke was horse crazy. She'd be thrilled about the rodeo this weekend.

Jasmine followed Mrs. Dalton's gaze, crow's feet bracketing the woman's blue eyes and deepening when she smiled. Her other daughter, a child as different from Gwen as fire was from ice, lifted a Breyer horse and pretended to make it jump over a wooden fence, staring at the thing as if it were real and she actually rode it. That was the difference between her two girls. Gwen was her cuddle-bunny, always smiling, chatting, happy to be with people. Brooke was always so serious, quiet, looking at the world as if she'd like to take it apart and put it back together again. They were exactly alike physically—blond hair, blue eyes, chubby little cheeks—but were completely different inside.

"Well, thanks for staying late tonight." Stupid helicopter ride had put her behind. "I appreciate it."

You enjoyed that ride. Come on. Admit it.

"My pleasure. They're good girls."

And she had enjoyed the ride. Surprisingly, she'd found it useful, too. She'd learned that the Baron rigs were all set up the same way. Pumps to the right. Parking area to the left. All painted a muted green. The little details that would allow her to replicate what she'd seen, and all thanks to Jet.

Her children would scare the heck out of a man like him.

"You ready for your baths?" she asked the girls, telling herself to put Jet—and work—out of her mind.

"Hooray. Bath," Gwen said, wiggling down from her arms.

"What time do you need me tomorrow?"

Jasmine met Mrs. Dalton's kind blue eyes. "Same as usual."

She followed the woman to the door, burying her hand in Gwen's hair. Her kids were all that mattered to her, not the gleam in Jet Baron's eyes.

She expected to see those eyes the next day, and she did, but only briefly. He passed in front of her office— hand waving, lips smiling—and then he was gone. Jasmine looked at the spot where he'd been and sank into her chair.

Handsome cuss. And he knew it, too.

Two minutes later the office's messaging program chimed a greeting.

Good morning, sunshine. Feeling better?

Heat buffeted her cheeks as if she'd just opened an oven door. She found herself glancing around, as though one of her coworkers might somehow glean that the boss's son had just called her "sunshine," although how that could be possible when she had her own office, Jasmine didn't know.

She told herself to ignore him and turned her attention back to the report she'd been updating. They'd already gotten a new bid on that gravel. She needed to put in the numbers.

Hello?

Don't respond.

You're ignoring me?

With a sigh of exasperation, she typed in I'm fine.

She didn't trust the man not to confront her face-to-face if she didn't reply—that's why she'd responded. But as she paged through the report, she kept glancing at that little box, waiting for his response. This was crazy. She was the mother of two. A professional businesswoman.

Bing!

You look fine, indeed.

"Wretched man."

"Who's wretched?"

Jasmine gasped, horrified to spot her boss standing in front of her. "Ms. Baron. Hello."

Were her cheeks as red as they felt? Had Lizzie seen her brother's message? Did she know how giddy and breathless and ridiculously pleased Jasmine suddenly felt?

"Mind if I have a seat?"

Lizzie Baron was the most elegant and refined woman Jasmine had ever met. She'd pulled her dark hair into a chignon. The black dress she wore looked impeccable—no oatmeal stains in sight. She'd covered it with a matching jacket, one that casually covered the growing mound in her belly. The woman oozed confidence and professionalism.

"Go ahead."

Blue eyes swept her office, resting on the framed picture behind her, just as her brother's gaze had done the day before. "Are those your twins?"

So Jet had been talking about her? She didn't know if that was a good thing or a bad thing.

"Yes."

"Can I see?"

Jasmine turned, scooping up the framed photograph and handing it to Lizzie Baron. The woman's eyes grew soft, a smile lifting the edges of her mouth.

"Adorable," her boss said.

"A handful," Jasmine admitted.

"I bet." The smile grew, and Jasmine found herself thinking yet again that she could really like this woman. She treated her like an equal, not a cog in the machine, and certainly not like an outsider in a man's world, which was how it'd been during her internships in college.

"Listen, I'll be quick."

Bing! Jasmine's eyes flicked to her computer screen.

Is my sister in there?

"Jet tells me you've had some tough luck."

Oh, dear God in heaven, the man *had* been talking about her.

"I know a little about what it's like to feel alone."

Bing!

Call her Lizard Face. She hates it.

"I just want you to know that we're a family-friendly company. If you ever feel overwhelmed and you think you might need some time off, you're free to do that, especially with all the late hours you've been working. We believe in flextime here."

Clearly, Jet had not only told his sister about the helicopter ride, but also about her breakdown.

"Thank you, Ms. Baron—"

"Lizzie," she quickly corrected.

"Lizzie, I'm really okay. One of my girls was restless the other evening and I didn't get enough sleep, but I slept like a log last night."

Lizzie studied her intently. Jasmine prayed the stupid instant message wouldn't chime.

"It can't be easy raising twins on your own."

What was this? The Baron family therapy hour? The thing was, the kindness in the woman's eyes created yet another lump in her throat.

"It hasn't been easy, Ms. Baron...Lizzie, but as the girls get older, it'll get better."

She looked like Jet. Not the eyes. They were as different from her brother's eyes as sapphires were from emeralds. It was the nose, and maybe the chin. That was all Brock Baron, but his children didn't have his eyes, at least not the ones she'd met. She wondered for a moment about their mother. Come to think of it, she'd never heard of the woman, just their stepmother, Julieta, who worked at Baron Energies, as well.

"I'm sure it will, but I wanted to reassure you that you're doing a great job. We're really pleased with how well you've acclimated to the job."

Jasmine straightened up in her chair, pleased. "Thank you."

Bing!
Don't look. Do not *look.*

Tell her she has spinach in her teeth.

The man was incorrigible. She should *not* be amused, and yet she wanted to smile.

"Listen. Jet said he told you about the benefit rodeo

this weekend. I really want to encourage you to come." She shifted in her chair, reached into the jacket that covered her stylish black dress. "I have four tickets here. I wasn't sure if maybe you were seeing someone or if you wanted to bring some help, but you should come. We do a big tri-tip barbecue afterward. There's lots of fun stuff for your girls to do, too. A petting zoo, pony rides, stick-horse races. You'll have a great time, plus it'll get you out of the office for a bit because don't think we haven't noticed you've been working weekends."

Jasmine froze in the act of taking the tickets from her boss's hand. An engagement ring caught the sun's rays. Spots of light danced on Jasmine's desk, but she hardly noticed because she was trying hard not to appear chagrined.

"J.C., I know what it's like to try to make it in a man's world." The smile she gave Jasmine was full of kindness. "I'm intimately familiar with what it's like, you know, to think you have to work longer hours, do more work, be better at your job than anyone else, but I hope you know it's not like that here. We're thrilled to have you. Please, take a break. Have some fun with your girls. I insist."

Jasmine took the tickets, then looked away. There it went again. Big, giant lump in the throat. Damn these Barons.

"I will."

"Good. We'll see you there, then."

Alas, part of that "we" meant Jet, and the way her stomach tingled, the way her heart sped up, well, that was the most disconcerting part of all.

Chapter Seven

"She's here."

Jet didn't pretend not to know which "she" his sister Savannah referred to. Still, he refused to turn around and look in Jasmine's direction. Instead, he pretended to be straightening up the display of pies and baked goods his sister had set out beneath a canvas awning attached to her latest investment—a portable concession stand with the words *The Peach Pit* emblazoned on the side.

"She's here? Good," he said dismissively.

"She's pretty." Savannah wedged herself between the table of goodies and him. From behind long bangs, Savannah's eyes sparkled in a way that rivaled the wedding ring on her finger. "You want me to call her over here for a slice of pie?"

He should never have told her about the coworker he'd befriended. Goodness knew why he had. He'd made it clear he wasn't interested in her, not in that way, but Savannah clearly thought otherwise. And all he needed was for Lizzie to catch wind of Savannah's thoughts on the matter, although the Baron Energies' vice president of operations hadn't been near Savannah's fund-raising bake sale the whole afternoon. Too busy playing hostess with the mostest. It seemed as if half of Dallas had shown up, the grandstands packed judging by the cheers he heard from time to time.

He shot Savannah a look. "I told you. It's not like that."

His sister narrowed her eyes, and the way she looked at him had him asking "What?" impatiently.

"Nothing."

Nothing his ass.

He was about to reiterate once more—and for the final time—that he was Jasmine Marks's *friend.* But Savannah had turned away, a wide smile on her face as she announced, "You must be J.C. Welcome to the Peach Pit Stop."

Jet wanted to groan. Could his sister be any more obvious? Jasmine would know they'd been talking about her. He quickly turned and opened his mouth to offer an excuse—

And couldn't speak.

Rational thought went up in a cloud of nuclear debris. She stood there, long, blond hair windblown around her face, two little girls—miniature bookends—on either side of her, their hands tucked into her own, pigtail braids the same platinum color as their mother's.

"Hey," she said with a smile.

She wore jeans and a dark blue button-down top and her eyes were warm and friendly and the same color as the sky, and Jet could have gone on staring at her for days. Except he couldn't. Shouldn't. There were two good reasons why a woman like her was all wrong for him, and they stood on either side of her. Two adorable reasons, he quickly amended.

Savannah poked him with an elbow.

"Hey," he croaked.

"Girls, say hello to Mr. Baron." She glanced down

at the twins, her thick hair falling over one shoulder, one curl in particular resting next to the shadow of her cleavage. "He's the one I told you about, the one who gave me a helicopter ride."

Open your mouth. Form words. *Talk.*

"Helicopter ride?" one of the little girls said, blue eyes exactly like Jasmine's instantly sparking to life. "Can you take me next?"

"A helicopter ride, eh?" echoed Savannah, one dark brow lifting, her expression clearly teasing.

"Gwen, you can't just invite yourself like that," Jasmine said.

"I can't?" The girl glanced at her mother. They had the same profile. The same chin. The same everything. The other twin, too, from what he could tell, although she'd buried her face behind her mother's leg.

"And who's this?" he finally managed to say.

"This is Brooke." Jasmine thrust her hand forward, forcing the little girl to come out from hiding. "Brooke, say hello."

From somewhere far away, the child uttered a single word, whispered in such a low register that canines would've had a hard time hearing her. "Hi."

He smiled, the strangest sensations unfurling near his heart. "Hello, girls." He turned to his sister. "I bet they'd like something sweet, Savannah. What do you say? My treat."

Savannah had the funniest look on her face. She'd been staring at him, he realized. Watching his face.

"Sure," his sister said slowly. "If their mom doesn't mind."

Mom, he repeated. Mother of two. Little girls with thoughts and feelings and hearts of their own and who would interfere with his dates with Jasmine and create havoc—

Whoa. Wait. What the hell was he thinking about *dates?*

"I don't mind at all." She looked down at her girls, sunlight framing her head and setting her hair aglow, the dark blue shirt she wore parting briefly and enough that he could see a hint of her breasts. She wore some kind of frilly bra. He could just make out the pattern of the lace before the gap closed again.

"How about a piece of my sister's famous peach pie?"

"That'd be great, huh, girls?" Jasmine asked.

Gwen's whole body just about wiggled in delight at the prospect of the treat. "Ooh," she said. "I *love* peach pie."

And the way she proclaimed it—as if pie was an integral part of her childhood—made Jet grin despite his sudden panic. Brooke, however, went back to hiding behind her mother's leg.

"Come on over here, girls," Savannah said, turning to the display table set up alongside the white trailer and scooping up a pie.

Alas, there seemed to be one thing guaranteed to prod Brooke out from behind her mother's leg, and that appeared to be a competitive nature. Whatever her sister wanted must be something she should have, too, because the moment Gwen moved toward the pie table, Brooke followed.

"Pick a piece," he heard Savannah say.

Jasmine watched, the smile still on her face, but when she noticed him staring at her, he saw that smile wobble a bit.

"They're adorable." And he meant it. Carbon copies

of their mom, right down to the smile, or at least Gwen's smile. "How do you tell them apart?"

She shrugged. "People ask me that all the time, but it's really easy for me. They're so different."

He eyed the two girls, thinking they weren't.

"Gwen has pudgier cheeks than Brooke," she explained. "Brooke is shorter, too."

"Brooke seems to be shyer."

"She is. I swear, where personality is concerned, they couldn't be more different."

She loved her kids. It was there in her eyes, in the way the smile changed from one of amusement to one of pride. He'd never met Darren, the man she'd been engaged to, although the oil industry was a small one, but he didn't see a speck of anyone but Jasmine in the twins' faces.

"That one!" an excited Gwen said, pointing toward—and darn near gouging in the process—a piece of the pie. "I want that one."

"And what about you?" his sister asked gently. "Which one would you like?"

Brooke just shrugged, the gesture an exact duplicate of her mother's right down to the same shoulder—and it made Jet chuckle.

"How about I pick one out for you?" his sister asked.

The little girl shrugged again.

"What's so funny?" Jasmine asked.

He looked her square in the eye. "She's you." He pointed. "A little Mini-Me, right down to the gestures."

"No, she's not."

"Yum," Gwen said, having been given her piece by Savannah. "Mommy, this is *soo* good. You should have a piece."

The plate she held wobbled precariously. Jasmine

rushed forward. So did Jet. They were just in time to save the pie from committing suicide.

"Better keep that on the table," Jasmine said, setting it back down.

"Here's your piece," Savannah said to Brooke, who eyed the fork as if she was afraid his sister might try to stab her with it.

"Go ahead," Jasmine said. "It's okay. Take it."

Clearly her desire for the treat outweighed the child's mistrust of his sister because she took the utensil and then gently scooped up a piece and the moment the gooey mess entered her mouth, her eyes widened and her brows lifted, as if that one bite contained all the best birthday presents, all her favorite Christmas presents, and all the tooth-fairy money in the world.

"I think you have a new fan," he told his sister.

"Do you like it?" Jasmine asked.

The little girl's nod was so enthusiastic Jet wondered if she'd hurt her neck.

"Of course she does," a new voice said, one Jet recognized. Lizzie. "Savannah's peach pie is the best in Texas."

"Ms. Baron," Jasmine said, a polite smile on her face.

Her sister smiled back. "I told you, it's Lizzie."

"My liege," Jet said, thumping his chest and tipping at the waist.

She rolled her eyes. "Knock it off, Jethro."

"Uh-oh." Savannah glanced between the two of them. "Nothing's guaranteed to get under Jet's skin faster than being called Jethro."

Jasmine's look said it all. *Jethro?*

"I'm glad you made it, J.C." Lizzie ignored her brother and sister. "Your girls are adorable."

"Thanks."

Lizzie would have her own little boy or girl to love before long, and Jet couldn't be happier for her. Yes, even though she'd just called him Jethro. Funny how quickly things had changed for their family. Lizzie and Carly engaged. Savannah married. Speaking of Carly, he'd been hoping to bump into her today. He wouldn't put it past his dad to ask for an update. When he glanced at Jasmine, he had the thought that maybe now would be a good time to leave, what with Lizzie watching him so closely.

"Has anyone seen Carly around?" he asked.

Savannah frowned. "I did earlier. I think she's over by the arena with Jacob and Chris setting up for the rough stock riding clinic."

The clinic. His other obligation today, although he wouldn't get together with the local high school boys until later. And girls, he swiftly amended. Carly would have his hide if he didn't remember there were girls competing these days, too.

"Jasmine, have you picked up your dinner tickets yet?" Savannah asked. She glanced at the covered tent across the way. Tables and chairs had been set up beneath it. "You should do that now instead of waiting until the rodeo's over when there's a big rush. You'll need one in order to eat."

"Oh." She glanced at Jet. "I didn't know."

"It's how we keep tabs on how many meals are served," he provided. "My sister Lizzie, ever the accountant."

"You should go right now," Savannah said. "Leave the twins here. Lizzie and I can watch them."

"Savannah," Lizzie growled.

"What?"

"She doesn't want to leave her kids with strangers."

"It's just for a second. Go with Jet," Savannah ordered. "We'll watch the girls while they finish eating their pie."

Jet would have laughed if he wasn't suddenly panicked at the thought of being alone with Jasmine. And if that scared him, he couldn't imagine what he'd feel like if he went on a date with her and the girls. Dating and kids—they didn't mix. Plus, he'd never been big on the fatherhood thing. Sure, he'd watched his little half brother, Alex, Brock and Julieta's son, from time to time, but that was different. Anna, their longtime cook and housekeeper, had always been within earshot.

Jasmine didn't appear to like the idea any better than him. She peered between his sisters and him, looking about as comfortable as a cat on a bull.

"Go on," Savannah said. "I insist."

There was no getting out of it now, not without sounding rude, but he shot Lizzie a glance that clearly conveyed his dismay. His sister's lips pressed together, but he couldn't exactly say no. Not without coming off sounding like a jerk. He had no choice but to play the host with the most, too. No choice at all.

The most beautiful woman on the rodeo grounds.

Yeah, she was. So what was wrong with him? He enjoyed the company of beautiful women. So what if she had kids? They could be friends.

Admit it. You want to be more than friends.

And he did, damn it. He really did.

Chapter Eight

She'd just left her twins with her boss and the woman's sister. Could she be any more unprofessional?

Jasmine glanced behind her. Both her girls were so engrossed in their pie, they hadn't even noticed she'd left. She didn't know how to feel about that. To be honest, she didn't know how to feel about anything lately. The girls would be okay. She knew that; it was Jet who had her flummoxed.

"Have you met Julieta yet?" he asked.

She couldn't focus. She had to replay his words to understand them, and even then she had to force herself to come up with a reply. He was 100 percent cowboy today in his light green button-down and his black hat that matched his jeans. And despite telling herself she shouldn't be noticing the way those jeans hugged his hips, his good looks made her as giddy as a prom date.

"No. Not yet." Brock Baron's wife, a woman not much older than her stepkids, but who was genuinely nice if office gossip was to be believed. She'd heard she was gorgeous, too.

They ducked beneath the shelter of the giant tent, one big enough to hold a wedding. It had dawned a warm, summer day, but the heat outside was nothing compared to the heat she felt standing next to Jet. She'd thought about him all night. Heck. She'd thought about him this morning, too, and on the way to the rodeo grounds.

"Hey, Maria," Jet said. "You seen Julieta?"

Maria was Brock's secretary and a woman Jasmine had met before. The woman was right in the middle of bundling napkins and cutlery, but she looked up with a bright smile on her face.

"Jet. Good to see you. And, yes, I have seen her. She's up in the grandstands with Alex watching the rodeo."

Jasmine glanced up at Jet in time to catch his megawatt smile, the one that made her toes curl and her stomach to do that strange little flip.

"I need dinner tickets for Jasmine and her little girls. Is that something you can help us with?"

Maria glanced between the two of them with an even brighter smile. "Of course." She turned to a nearby three-ring binder, marking something on a sheet of paper inside it before handing Jasmine some purple tickets.

"Just give this to your server," she said, her brown eyes glancing between the two of them again as she shoved a hank of black hair behind her ears. "Get here early. These high school kids eat like they haven't seen food in a year."

"Will do," Jet answered for her.

She needed to get away from Jet. Nothing reinforced the thought more than the way Maria looked at the two of them, as if she were judging whether or not they could be a couple. It created an awkwardness within her she hadn't felt in...well, in a long, long time.

"Thanks," she told the woman.

She needed to get back to her girls, back to the comfort of their arms—away from the confusion of Jet. She glanced in their direction, but they were still eating their pie while Savannah and Lizzie stared after her and Jet. Jasmine's ears began to burn.

Wrong. All wrong. She knew that. The man didn't take his own family business seriously. Why the hell was she so attracted to him? She didn't have time for an affair, not that he'd given any indication he was interested in her that way.

Firming her resolve, she tucked the tickets Maria gave her in her pocket and headed back to her girls. Jet didn't seem to mind. In fact, he seemed a little distracted.

"Mommy, look! Horses!"

It was Brooke who'd spoken, of course. Brooke who stared with longing at the horses.

"Can I pet one?" she asked the adults around her.

"Sure," Savannah said. "You can even ride them. Jet will take you over there."

Jasmine watched as Lizzie's brows reached all the way to her hairline when she turned to her sister. Clearly, she didn't like the idea of Savannah pushing them to spend more time together, and that's what she was doing. No doubt about it, though goodness knew why.

"It's okay," Jasmine quickly said. "I can take them."

Was Jet red around the neckline? Where had the winking smiles gone?

"Don't be ridiculous," he said brusquely. "What kind of boss would I be if I didn't introduce them to horses?"

He was her boss. Well, sort of. And so was his sister. And despite how nice that sister was, Jasmine might blow the whole deal if she started making googly eyes at Ms. Baron's little brother.

"Really, Jet, it's okay."

But Brooke had already sneaked up on him and taken his hand. Gwen had thrust her hand into her own. Jasmine absently glanced at Savannah and Lizzie. Savannah made a shooing motion. Lizzie frowned.

And that was how she found herself following Jet Baron to the pony rides where he helped settle first Brooke and then Gwen onto the back of an animal. She could tell he was a bit tentative at first. When he lifted Brooke it was as if he hoisted a piece of glass. The man in charge of the pony rides, Jet's sister Carly's fiancé, Luke, she'd been told, smiled at them kindly and told her she could walk alongside her daughter if she wanted. One of Jet's stepbrothers, Daniel, helped out. It was crazy trying to keep all of Jet's family members straight. The only reason she knew she'd remember Daniel's name was because he looked just like his brother, Jacob, a man Jasmine had met at the office. Jacob worked for Baron Energies, too.

"We ready?" Luke asked.

"Let's go," Brooke ordered.

And so began round after round after round of loops along the perimeter of the tiny corral. Clearly, there was no time limit. Jasmine became convinced they would have been there all day if not for the fact that some other kids showed up.

That's when the trouble began.

"Time to get down, honey," she heard Jet say.

"No."

Jasmine had already hoisted Gwen down. Her eldest daughter had all but jumped off on her own. Clearly, she didn't feel the same passion about horses that Brooke did.

"Brooke." She grabbed Gwen's hand and turned toward the younger twin. "Mr. Baron asked you to get down. It's someone else's turn."

She knew in an instant that what was coming

wouldn't be pretty. Brooke's pale skin had begun to turn red, a sure sign of impending temper.

"No!"

"Now, come on," Jasmine heard Jet say. "I'll help you."

The moment he touched her daughter's sides Brooke screamed. Loudly. Jasmine had never been more mortified in her life. Jet let go and stepped back. It was as if her daughter had turned into a rattlesnake. She saw the fear in his eyes. Maybe not fear. More like...dismay.

"Brooke Marks! You stop your screaming now."

She thrust Gwen toward Jet, then reached for Brooke who stubbornly refused to move. Her daughter might be riding a pony, but Brooke was writhing around so much Jasmine felt as if she were wrestling a wet fish.

"Here."

It was a masculine voice but not Jet's. No. It was Jet's soon-to-be brother-in-law.

"Quiet now, honey," Luke said, his brown eyes filled with patience and understanding. "You can ride again in a few minutes."

"No!" Brooke all but screamed. "No, no, no. She won't let me."

Jasmine was sure her face turned as red as the checkers on a table cloth. "Yes, I will," Jasmine said even though she suspected she'd just been expertly manipulated by her four-year-old daughter. "You can ride again later on."

"But the ponies will be gone." Her daughter had started to cry, big dramatic sobs that had Jasmine glancing around in embarrassment.

"No, they won't," said the man in the Stetson hat. "They'll be right here, and if I do have to take them away for some reason, I'm sure Jet can bring you out to his place to ride his horses tomorrow or the next day."

A glance at Jet revealed his look of surprise. For some reason his expression disappointed her. Stupid, ridiculous reaction. After all the times she'd warned herself away.

"I'm sure that won't be necessary," she said.

If ever she needed proof that Jet Baron was absolutely the worst man in the world for her, this was it. He stood back, holding Gwen's hand, looking for all the world like a man who'd stepped on hot coals. There was nothing even remotely fatherly about him. Far from it. This was a man who didn't know the first thing about children, or how to appease them when they were upset, or how to comfort them in their time of need.

"I want to ride Jet's horses," Brooke pronounced, some of the color fading from her cheeks. At last she allowed Luke, a man who clearly knew a thing or two about children, to lower her to the ground. "Jet has big horses, not ponies."

"Yes, he does." The cowboy seemed amused. "He has lots of big horses and I'm sure he'd love to show them to you sometime."

No, he would not. It was clear he didn't want a thing to do with her or her kids.

It stung.

"Yeah, sure," Jet said, but it was too little, too late. He scooted forward with Gwen. "You can come over to my house anytime you want."

Brooke wiped her eyes. "I want to ride the big horses."

"Okay," Jet said. "Okay. We can do that."

They could, but would not. Jasmine would make certain of that.

"MAN, THAT WAS a close call," Luke said. They stood side by side as they watched Jasmine and her kids walk away. "I thought for sure that little girl was going to bring the cops with her screams."

"Is that normal?" Jet asked.

Luke's eyes flashed amusement. "For little girls? Yes. I'm learning they're drama queens from a young age." His future brother-in-law clapped him on the back. "Welcome to the world of kids."

Jeez. What was with everyone? "She's not my girl-friend."

Luke drew back. "No?"

"No."

"Really? With her looks I thought for sure she'd be your type."

"She has kids."

"So?"

Yeah, so? asked a little voice. He'd been riding fif-teen-hundred-pound bulls nearly his entire life. He wasn't afraid of fifty pounds of sugar and spice and ev-erything nice now, was he?

"It'd be complicated."

Luke's brown eyes sparked. "The best things in life are."

Jet just shook his head. "Speaking of complicated, you seen your fiancée around? I need to talk to her about something."

"As a matter of fact, I have. She's over by the buck-ing chutes. She's pulling rope for one of the girls today."

"One of?"

"Yup. There's more than one."

Times had changed. Of course, women still weren't allowed to ride in the PRCA—that might be a long time coming, but they were allowed to ride high school rodeo,

like today. If they wanted to ride more than that they
had to stick with the Women's Professional Rodeo Association.

"I should have known she'd be over there supporting her protégée."

"You know your sister well."

Not all that well if she were off searching for their
mother without him knowing it. To be honest he was
kind of glad to finally get to the bottom of things. His
dad's words had been weighing on his mind.

The Loving County rodeo grounds followed the same
blueprint as other facilities with similar names across
the United States. One side of the square lot hosted the
arena. On one side of that arena were the grandstands,
the other side the chutes for the livestock, and behind
it all a place for friends and family to hang out. Baron
Energies sponsored the event every year. It wasn't just
a rodeo competition, but a way for their alma mater to
raise money. Giving back, and they were happy to do it.

He spotted two familiar faces once he climbed over
the alleyways that surrounded the chute.

"You guys taking notes?" he asked his brother Jacob
and his future brother-in-law Chris. "Figuring out which
kids need the most help?"

"Yup," Jacob said. "And we could use your help."

His big brother—technically stepbrother—always
took things so seriously. He probably really did have
notes on all the kids riding in the clinic today.

"Sorry. I promised Dad I'd talked to Carly about
something." He turned to his future brother-in-law, the
tall cowboy looking right at home behind the chutes.
Not surprising. He'd met Lizzie at a rodeo. Well, after
a rodeo when he'd been nursing a beer after getting
bucked off a bronc—or so the story went. His brown

hair was covered by a black cowboy hat similar to his own, his brown eyes filled with warmth.

"Uh-oh. That sounds serious."

"It's nothing. Not really." He smiled and excused himself.

He found Carly right where he expected. Bull riding wasn't until the very end of the day and so Carly stood near the crowd of female competitors.

"I've been looking for you."

Carly swung toward him, a smile on her face, blue eyes full of excitement. She loved rodeos. His dad often said if she'd been born a man she'd have made it to the NFR.

"Hail the conquering hero." She glanced at the girls around her. "Gals, this is Jet, my brother."

"We know who he is," said one of the girls, her lavender eyes full of hero worship, something Jet tried to rebuff with a polite smile. To be honest, being behind the chutes made him antsy. It was why he'd been helping Savannah at her booth earlier. He'd known it would be hard to stand there and watch when he wanted to be riding instead. Alas, that was an itch he would need to quell, at least until Lizzie had her baby. He'd be lucky to get to one or two rodeos over the next couple months.

He met Carly's gaze again. "Can I talk to you for a moment?"

"About what?"

He glanced at Alyssa. "Something personal."

Carly flicked her blond ponytail behind her as she said, "Sure."

She guided him away from the cowboys and cowgirls, still behind the chutes but out of earshot. When she turned to face him the noonday sun hit her eyes, turning them a light, light blue.

"What is it?"

"What's this I hear about you searching for our mom?" he returned.

Any doubt he might have had that his dad had gotten some bad information faded the moment he spotted the telltale signs of guilt in his sister's eyes.

"Heard about that, have you?"

"I did, although I won't tell you how. I am curious, however, who else knows."

If she was curious about his source, she held her tongue. "Lizzie and Savannah. Chris, Travis and Luke, of course."

Good Lord. Was there anybody who didn't know?

"What the hell are you guys looking for her for?"

Carly shrugged. "Savannah started it. She brought Lizzie into the picture when Savannah had her health scare, and then me. Travis is helping with the search."

Travis, Savannah's new husband. It made sense. The man was a P.I.

"You close to finding her?"

She shook her head. "It's like a maze. We think we're getting somewhere and then it's a dead end, so we try a different tack, only that doesn't work, either. I'm beginning to wonder if we'll ever find her."

Behind them the crowd cheered again. Someone must have covered the bronc they were riding. It made him wish he was out there, too, instead facing his sister and spying for his dad.

"What happens if you do find her? You guys ever think about that?"

"I don't know. I think we're all just curious. Why did she leave us, Jet? Why did she just take off like she did? I know you don't remember much of that. You were so young, but most of us do. I remember the desserts she used to make, and crying when she left." She shook her head, her expression pained. "It haunts me. I think it haunts Savannah and Lizzie, too."

No matter how much he might disapprove, he couldn't deny their reasoning. Carly was right. He didn't remember a thing. Honestly, he'd thought of Peggy as his mother. He thought about her a lot. Her death was part of the reason why he'd thrown himself into rodeo. You had to focus when you were riding bulls. It'd helped him through the grief of losing his stepmother.

"Well, I guess I wish you luck, then."

Carly tipped her head and stared up at him. "Aren't you curious?"

He stroked his chin in thought. The smell of the tri-tip barbecue wafted over to them, reminding him they still had dinner to get through.

"No," he admitted. "Not really. Sure, I wonder why she left from time to time, but I didn't know the woman. If she walked up to me today I wouldn't recognize her." It was his turn to shrug. "I think you guys should be careful, though. If you do find her, think long and hard before you rush off to meet her."

"Why do you say that?"

He thought for a moment, then said, "Things like this don't always work out. You've seen the television shows, the ones where the people try to find their birth parents. Sometimes it works out, more often than not, it doesn't. Just don't get your hopes up."

"So I guess you have no interest in helping us?"

He shook his head. "Not really."

He thought of Jasmine then for some reason, of how helpless he'd felt when Brooke had refused to get off the horse, and how much he'd wanted to please the little girl.

How could his mom have left them?

He wasn't even Brooke's father and the need to please, to help that little girl, had surprised him. He supposed he should have them out to his ranch. That wouldn't go over well with Lizzie, but it couldn't be helped. A promise was a promise.

"I'll let you know if we find her," Carly said.

"Do that." He could decide then if he wanted to tell their dad, but as he thought back to the look on his dad's face he began to wonder if there was more to his interest in their search than he was letting on. He almost mentioned it to Carly, but he couldn't do that, not without tipping his hand. Besides, he had bigger fish to fry.

What in the heck was he going to do about Jasmine?

Chapter Nine

"We need to talk."

Jet shut down his email at the same time he glanced at the clock on his computer monitor. "Can we do it later?" he asked his sister. "I'm supposed to meet the aggregate contractor out at the job site in a half hour."

Lizzie plopped down in the chair opposite his desk, and Jet recognized the look on her face. "What'd I do wrong?"

"Nothing, really. You're doing a great job as a project manager."

Surprisingly.

That was the unspoken word. He leaned back in his seat, the chair rolling back a bit. "Wow. Praise from my liege. Color me happy."

"Will you stop calling me that?"

He tried like the devil not to smile, but the damn thing slipped past his guard, anyway. "Sorry. It's just so fitting."

"Yeah, well, too bad Dad doesn't feel the same way."

His smile faded. He hated being reminded of the fact that Brock wanted him to take over Baron Energies when Lizzie was clearly the better man...or woman as the case may be.

"So if it's not my performance on the job, what is it?"

She frowned. He knew. In that moment, he knew.

"Not Jasmine again."

His sister released a huff of impatience. "Yes, J.C. again. I heard you invited her kids out to your place to ride."

"Yes, but it wasn't my fault. It was Luke who made the suggestion. I'd look like a chump if I didn't agree."

"Don't do it."

Unfortunately, he knew she was right. He shook his head, a bird flying by the window outside catching his attention. It soared on an updraft for a moment—Jet admiring its freedom—before stroking its wings in a way that lifted it up and out of sight.

"I like her."

"Clearly."

"And I feel sorry for her."

"There's a difference between feeling sorry and getting involved, and you, sir, are on your way to getting involved."

He opened his mouth to deny it, but could he really? He kept telling himself she wasn't his type, that her kids scared the hell out of him, yet he couldn't stop thinking about her. Yeah, he might have panicked a bit when Brooke had her fit, but it didn't change the fact that he'd sincerely wanted to please the little girl with every fiber of his being. It had scared him how much he wanted to soothe her ruffled feathers. That's why he'd looked at Jasmine with such panic, why his conversation with Carly had upset him later.

"I hear you're looking for our mom."

As a change of subject, it was a doozy. Lizzie couldn't appear more shocked.

"How'd you hear about that?"

He shrugged. "I was talking to Carly about it."

Not really a lie. Not exactly the truth, either.

"And do you disapprove?"

Jet took a deep breath. "I'm going to tell you what I told Carly. Be careful. I worry about you girls getting hurt. The woman already rejected us once. It'll sting if she does it again."

Lizzie eyed him intently before saying, "Duly noted." Then she turned the table on him. "Now, about J.C."

"You have nothing to worry about," he said. "I swear." He held up his hands. "She's a friend and a co-worker. That's all there is to it. I have no amorous feelings toward Jasmine Marks, I mean J. C. Marks."

His sister lifted a brow.

"I swear."

Liar, liar pants on fire.

The truth was he found Jasmine incredibly attractive. Her twins, well, he supposed they would take some getting used to, but if he really liked Jasmine, there was no reason to let them get in the way.

If he really liked Jasmine.

When he looked back at his sister he realized she still stared at him. He felt his neck begin to color. She knew he wasn't telling the truth—of course she knew. Heck, his sister had been the one to figure out he'd been the one to leave the pasture gate open when he was nine, thereby allowing a few dozen head of cattle to escape down the road. To this day he had no idea how she'd figured it out.

"Be careful, Jet."

"You've got nothing to worry about."

He had himself well in control, he reassured himself as he drove out to the job site a few minutes later. What he hadn't told Lizzie was that Jasmine would be there, too. He hadn't seen her since the rodeo. That was three days ago and if he didn't know better, he would swear she'd been avoiding him, but that wasn't possible. He was reasonably certain she liked him and so she had no cause to avoid him.

Unless....

Nah. She wasn't attracted to him, too, was she? Sure, she might like him, but like him like him? Like him like *that?* He supposed it was possible. He'd always been able to charm the socks of women. Neither of his stepmothers had been immune to him, nor were his sisters, but what if Jasmine did like him? Like him like *that.* What if beneath the soft stares and gentle smile beat the heart of a woman who wanted more from him than a shoulder to cry on? Was he up for that?

He was still chewing the thought over as he turned onto a dusty strip of land marked by nothing more than a rusty barbwire fence and a keeled-over mailbox. Texas could be as flat as a blacksmith's anvil and this part west of Dallas was no exception. Prairie grass mixed with the occasional prickly pear cactus, and, even less frequently, the occasional cottonwood tree. A lot of nothing, most people would think. It was what was underneath that counted.

She was right where he'd first spotted her, only instead of her usual black dress and jacket, she wore jeans and a black Baron Energies polo shirt that matched his own corporate attire. Funny the contradictions he felt as he drove up to where she stood outside her truck, her long, blond hair tucked back in a ponytail. He admired her can-do attitude and yet worried about how hard she was working. The afternoon sun beat down on her form and it illuminated the pallor of her face. She appeared more tired than she had on Saturday, and he wondered if she'd had another rough night with one of the girls.

YOUR PARTICIPATION IS REQUESTED!

Dear Reader,

Since you are a lover of our books – we would like to get to know you!

Inside you will find a short Reader's Survey. Sharing your answers with us will help our editorial staff understand who you are and what activities you enjoy.

To thank you for your participation, we would like to send you 2 books and 2 gifts – **ABSOLUTELY FREE!**

Enjoy your gifts with our appreciation,

Pam Powers

**SEE INSIDE
FOR READER'S
SURVEY**

For Your Reading Pleasure...

We'll send you 2 books and 2 gifts
ABSOLUTELY FREE
just for completing our Reader's Survey!

He didn't have time to ask her because beside her was another truck and a big, burly man Jet recognized as the man they were supposed to meet.

They spent the next hour going over where things like aggregate rock and sand and lime were to be delivered, followed by a heated debate over the depth of the road base. Once again he found himself admiring Jasmine's smarts. She came up with the idea to use two types of rock, one less expensive than the other, to use for their road. It'd cut their cost by half.

When they said goodbye to the contractor, Jet was half tempted to clap her on the back in appreciation except he was afraid if he did, he'd knock her down. She seemed that tired. He'd watched as numerous times during their conversation she'd stifled a yawn.

"You look exhausted."

She glanced up from the notes she'd been taking. "Thanks." And he could hear the sarcasm in her tone.

"Another late night?"

She nodded, but something about the way her mouth flattened, about the way she didn't look up at him again, set alarm bells ringing.

"What wrong?"

She shook her head. "I'll be sure to send you a copy of my notes tomorrow."

"Jasmine, what's wrong?"

When she still wouldn't answer he tried to take her tablet out of her hands. She wouldn't let him, hiding it behind her back, but that only brought him closer, their bodies brushing.

Her eyes connected with his own.

And he knew. He knew that his hypothesis was true. She *did* like him—as in, she found him attractive. He should be flattered. Instead, what he felt was more akin

to dread and damned if he knew why. His sister must
have really put the fear of God into him.

When had he ever listened to his sister?

He grabbed the tablet, set it down on the edge of her
truck bed. He knew his next move would give his sister an anxiety attack if she ever found out, but he didn't
care. His hand, the one he'd used to set down the tablet, found Jasmine's shoulder. He placed it there, gently,
softly drawing her closer to him. And just as he suspected, the connection they shared, the chemistry between them, burst like a supernova, and it stunned him.
He lost the ability to breathe. When his chest finally
decompressed it caught her scent. Roses. She smelled
like a botanical garden, and he could have stood there
holding her all day. Instead, he pulled her closer, rested
a hand against the back of her head and snuggled her
close. She resisted at first. Of course she did. No strong,
independent woman would accept the aid of a man—
not for a second time.

"You don't have to do this alone, you know." He ignored the urge to nuzzle her hair with his nose. Lord,
he wanted to do that. "Sometimes it's okay to lean on
friends."

"Friends?" She drew back. "Is that what we are?"

He drew back, too. "Of course."

Damn it. He was going to do it. He was going to do
something stupid, something he knew he shouldn't do.

"Why do I have the feeling you just lied?"

"Because you're right. I did lie."

He leaned toward her, but he did it slowly so as not to
spook her. And even though he knew he took a terrible
risk even just holding her—sheesh, he was the poster
child for a sexual harassment lawsuit—he did it, anyway. He placed a kiss on her lips.

He thought he heard her gasp. Thought she might have straightened a few inches. He worried she might pull back, but she didn't. Instead, the strong, competent woman that was Jasmine Marks turned to mush in his arms. He had to prop her up against the truck, but that was okay because it brought their bodies closer—thigh touched thigh, hip touched hip, chest touched chest.

Lizzie's going to kill you.

He used his lower lip to gently nuzzle her own lips open, gently seeking, asking without words if she would let him taste her.

She said yes.

Like a punch to the gut—that's how it felt when she opened her mouth. His world tipped sideways. His heart stopped beating. She was warm inside and she tasted like coffee and maybe vanilla or mocha and she was responsive, tipping her head sideways and touching her tongue to his own. Her mouth was as soft as powdered sugar and just as sweet.

Good Lord.

He kissed her harder, and thought he could have stayed like that forever because tasting her was like getting the answer to a puzzle he hadn't even known existed. Alas, sanity prevailed and he knew. He just knew he had to pull back.

"Damn," he heard himself say.

He began to breathe once they were parted. His lungs sucked in deep gasps. He had to step away, to stop touching her so he could start thinking again.

"Damn," he said again.

"Jet."

"No." He placed his hands on his hips and stared at the ground because if he looked into her eyes he knew he'd want to kiss her again. "This was my fault. I shouldn't have touched you." He scrubbed a hand over his face. "Crap, my sister is going to kill me."

"Your sister would want to kill us both." She stepped forward and peered up at him. "It takes two to tango, Jet, and I didn't exactly fight you off."

"Because I didn't give you a chance. Damn, I am such an idiot. Look, if you want me to tell my sister I'm just not cut out for a desk job, I'll do that. I'll understand if you don't want to work with me."

"Don't be ridiculous." She lifted her chin up, her ponytail brushing her shoulder. "The last thing I need is more stress in my life because no matter what you say to your sister, she's going to blame me somehow. She's not stupid, you know. I saw the way she was looking at us. If she thinks I made a play for you or something, I'm toast. She'll never fully trust me again."

"What do you mean, more stress?"

Her eyes shifted away from him. "Nothing. I don't want you to quit."

"What's going on, Jasmine? I could tell earlier something's upset you."

"It's nothing." She put up the equivalent of a brick wall between them by stepping away and crossing to the tailgate area of her truck. "Just promise me you won't quit, okay?"

"All right, fine, I won't. What's wrong?"

"Nothing." And she released the word on a huff of utter exasperation.

He leaned toward her and glared.

"Okay, fine. I'm just tired, that's all. Being a full-time mom and a full-time engineer is a lot of work."

She was lying. Well, okay, maybe not lying. She didn't want to trust him with the truth.

"Is it the twins? Is something wrong with one of them?"

She jerked. "How in the heck could you know that?"

"I just know. It's written on your face. You look the epitome of a terrified mom right now."

He saw her lower lip tremble. She bit down on it before saying, "It's nothing. Brooke hasn't been feeling well lately, is all. I took her to the doctor a few weeks ago and they said it was nothing, but she's still not better. And you saw her at the rodeo on Saturday. She had a fit and that's not like her. On Sunday I could tell she wasn't well again so I took her back to the doctor and he said he still thinks it's a virus but they drew some blood so they could confirm that's all it is, but I still worry that it might be... That she might, you know, have something..."

"Really wrong with her," he finished for her.

She shook her head as if denying the thought to herself. "I'm waiting to hear back on the results, but I'm sure the pediatrician is right. It's just a little bug. Or she's growing. That's all. No big deal."

No big deal?

Was she insane? Her kid was sick. He might not be a father, but he had enough siblings to know what it felt like when someone you loved had a medical issue. Hell, Lizzie had scared the heck out of them a few months back when she'd had a problem with her pregnancy. And then he'd just recently heard Savannah had found a lump in her breast, but that had turned out to be nothing, too, thank God. Still, he knew the fear she must be feeling. The bitch of it was, he wanted to go to her, wanted to comfort her, only if he did that, he knew he'd be crossing the line. Again.

"It's all right, Jet." She nodded as if trying to reassure him, but he knew she only tried to comfort herself. "No need to look at me like that. I'll be okay. This won't affect my performance on the job."

"Of course it won't. You're a professional, Jasmine. I know that."

But she was terrified. And all alone. Wanting someone to lean on. He could see it in her eyes, and it broke his heart.

To hell with it.

He crossed to her again, reached for her once more, a part of him hoping she'd step back, but she didn't. Instead, she stared up at him with her big blue eyes and he knew, he just knew, he was lost.

"Come here." He wrapped his arms around her. She let him. He didn't try to kiss her, although damned if the moment he touched her he didn't want to do exactly that. Instead, he rested his head against her, inhaling her rosy essence.

"It's going to be okay," he said.

"I know."

He could tell she fought back tears, but she didn't let them fall. Oh, no. Not Jasmine. He somehow sensed it would be a long time before she broke down in front of him again—if ever.

"It's like you said, kids get sick, sometimes for weeks. It happens."

"I know."

But she was still terrified, which made him think her daughter's symptoms must have been out of the ordinary. She might not cry, but her body trembled, and he could feel the thrust of her heart as it beat against his own chest.

"When will you hear back?"

"They said tomorrow."

"And you're going to be a nervous wreck until then."

He felt her nod. "You know I am."

Something welled up from deep inside him, something that made him say, "You asked me earlier if we're friends and we are, Jasmine. I'm your friend. If you need to talk, I'm here for you. I promise I'll do whatever I can to help you. All you have to do is ask."

"I know, Jet, I'm just not certain how wise it would be to let things go any further than…this."

"Because of my sister."

"Yes, your sister," she echoed. "I know she doesn't approve of our, um, friendship."

Some things his sister didn't need to know about.

"Don't you worry about Lizzie. I can handle her."

He hoped.

Because the sad truth was, his sister ran the show. His dad might want him to take over, but they were a long way from that, if they ever got that far.

But he was nothing if not honest with himself. He liked Jasmine. Hell, he *more* than liked her. Lizzie would just have to deal.

"It's not just your sister, it's everything." She took a step back. "I have to go, but thanks, Jet. Thanks for being my…friend."

She didn't give him time to reply, and he knew she was putting the kibosh on any further dealings with him. Funny, he should be okay with that. He was well aware of all the reasons why he should avoid getting involved with her. He should take the easy out and let her go.

But as he watched her drive away, he wondered, wondered what it would be like to date a woman like her. Someone bright and beautiful and, yes, who had two kids. He realized if he did he wouldn't be dating just Jasmine. In a way he'd be dating her kids, too. He would be taking on the responsibility of not one, but three hearts.

He just wasn't certain he was man enough for the task.

Chapter Ten

She didn't sleep all night, and not just because she worried about her child. No. There was that kiss. The proof that she was kidding herself as far as Jet was concerned. Yes, he was a nice man, but there was this other thing, too. This hum of an undercurrent that sparked to life whenever he was near. And that kiss. That kiss had completely ruined whatever defensive wall she'd thought she could hide behind. Stupid, ridiculous, impulsive man.

"Momma, I don't feel good."

Any thoughts of Jet instantly evaporated when she caught sight of Brooke's pale face, her big blue eyes peeping out from behind her bedroom door, dark circles beneath her eyes.

"Hey, pumpkin, come into bed with Mommy."

Her daughter shuffled along in her Disney Princess pj's, and though the sun poked lazy fingers through Jasmine's bedroom window, she could still spot the paleness of her cheeks. Sparks of nausea-inducing fear shot through her nerve endings all over again.

"You still feeling bad?"

Her little girl nodded as she climbed beneath the covers. Jasmine pulled her up against her, burying her nose in her hair and inhaling the sweet scent of baby shampoo.

"Is it your tummy again?"

She felt more than saw her daughter nod in the room's dusky half-light. She'd been complaining of hunger a lot, and of being tired, but the odd thing was, no matter how much she ate—like that whole piece of pie at the rodeo the other day—she'd been losing weight. She'd been cranky, too, as evidenced by her meltdown over the horse. No matter how many hours Brooke slept Jasmine seemed to spend half her time trying to keep her from having a temper tantrum, and always over something completely stupid—like her Band-Aid not sticking to her finger, or getting off a pony.

She's just growing. It's probably nothing.

"Try to get a little more sleep," she said softly.

Her daughter quieted, as Jasmine wondered what the day would bring. She'd never been the Pollyanna type, even before all the sadness that had visited her life. She preferred being pragmatic. That's why she'd become an engineer. Math was black-and-white. When you calculated risk, you reduced the chances of a negative outcome. Ironic that she'd ended up with a man who didn't know the meaning of keeping himself safe. And before that, a father who had lived a life of reckless abandon. It didn't take a doctor to figure out that's probably why she was the way she was. Still, she'd had a great childhood. Her father had taught her how to be independent and that anything was possible. Then she'd lost him, and after that, there'd been Darren, yet another man who had spent his life flying in the face of fear, and now he was gone, too. She'd been left with a permanent reminder of what happened when you did something reckless and impulsive—like fall in love with a man who lived life as if it were one big adventure—and she wasn't only talking about Darren.

She woke up to the sound of someone knocking on the door. It took her a moment to get her bearings and to realize it was Mrs. Dalton. Brooke still slept next to her.

Brooke. The doctor.

She shot up so fast she woke up Brooke, who immediately started to cry. Of course.

"Shh," she soothed.

The morning didn't get any better from there. By the time she pulled into a parking spot beneath the Baron Energies building she was frazzled and felt as frayed as the end of a rope, one she held on to as she dangled over the edge of a cliff. She was a half hour late, again, and she'd had to pile her hair on top of her head because she hadn't had time to style it, and she was pretty sure there was a run in her nylons. She could feel it creeping up her ankle. She really shouldn't take her frustration with the world out on a hapless elevator button, but she stabbed the thing multiple times before tipping her head back and praying for the strength to make it through the day.

Something was wrong with her baby.

She didn't want to think about it, *couldn't* think about it. This was work, she thought as she walked past the receptionist. Her personal life couldn't interfere with her job.

"Tough morning?"

She froze by the entrance to her office. Jet walked toward her, the man looking as out of place in the corporate hallway as a quarterback amid a team of cheerleaders. She spotted an assistant take one glance at his denim-clad rear and dusty cowboy hat and nearly stop in her tracks. And that was a view of the rear. The front was even more devastating to her equilibrium. Clearly, he'd come from his father's ranch. Just as clearly, he hadn't bothered to change. She could smell the dust and sweat on him.

He glanced down and spread his arms. "Early-morning roping practice with my friends." He shrugged as if in apology. "Got to get ready for this weekend's rodeo. No time to change."

She nodded and slipped into her office before he could repeat his question, but just as she was about to close her door, he followed her inside, closing it behind them. "Have you heard yet?"

She shook her head. "Not yet." She glanced at her phone, looking to see if the message-waiting light blinked, but it held its amber-colored silence.

"You look tired."

"Thanks."

"Not in a bad way. I like your hair up like that."

Time to retreat. She scooted behind her desk before he did something they would both regret—like pull her into his arms again.

She could use a hug this morning.

Instead, she sat in her chair with a creak of metal and the sound of rolling wheels on the plastic mat beneath her desk. She clicked on her computer and attempted to look focused even though inside her head she was any-thing but. Sleep deprivation. Fear. Frustration. It rolled around inside of her, getting bigger and bigger until she was almost ill from the size of it. She hoped he wouldn't notice and logged in to her email, thinking he'd go away if she ignored him.

She should be so lucky.

"Maybe you should take the day off."

Her fingers froze over the keyboard. "I am not tak-ing the day off."

The man didn't get it. Then again, why would he?

He'd been born into a life of privilege. To him, everything came easily. If he wanted to take off, or if he wanted to come into the office late, he did.

"Go home and be with your girls while you…wait."

"About my girls and this weekend. That whole horse-riding thing. I know you didn't really want to do it in the first place and so I think we should cancel, especially with what's going on with Brooke."

She'd been trying to come up with a graceful way to bow out of that since their kiss. Being alone with him. Spending more time with him away from the office—bad idea.

"Of course." And she could have sworn she spotted a hint of relief. "We'll do it some other time."

Yeah. Some other time.

Why did his response disappoint her so much? She shouldn't want to be with him. She should keep her distance from him especially since the sight of him standing there, all rugged male cowboy, was enough to stir any woman's senses.

"In the meantime," he asked, "do you need some help? I can take over for you on some items if you want."

"That won't be necessary." She could handle work and whatever might be wrong with her daughter. She'd handled far worse. "I've got it all under control."

Or so she thought.

Because in the next instant the phone rang, and a glance at the caller ID revealed the doctor's office. Her heart froze and for a moment she didn't want to answer. Maybe she shouldn't. Maybe she should ignore it until Jet left. Or was that being cowardly?

"J. C. Marks," she answered, acutely aware of Jet sitting there, watching her. She wondered if he'd spotted the name on the caller ID, too.

"Ms. Marks, this is Renee from Dr. Lee's office. I'm calling to set up a time to go over the results of Brooke's blood work."

"Can you give it to me now?"

She knew the answer before the woman spoke. "No. I'm sorry. Dr. Lee wants to see you."

Oh, no. She knew what that meant.

She turned partly away from Jet. "I was told Dr. Lee would call me with the results."

She could hear typing in the background. Clearly, the woman on the other end was trying to think about how best to phrase her words without sending the mother of a patient into a panic.

Too late.

"Under certain circumstances that would happen," the woman finally said, "but not in this instance."

Because there was a problem.

Her world tilted. Jasmine's heart stopped beating. Dear God in heaven, what was wrong with her daughter?

"When did you want me to come in?"

No hesitation this time. "Today, if possible."

She couldn't breathe, closed her eyes, prayed for strength and said, "What time?"

"Well, if you could come in right now, that'd be great. Otherwise, we have an opening around 4:00 p.m."

To spend the day wondering? To sit at her desk all day and worry about what the problem might be? To probably spend most of the day researching Brooke's symptoms all the while praying and hoping it was nothing serious? No thanks.

"I'll be right over."

"Great. We'll see you shortly."

She hung up, took a moment to compose herself, then

turned to face Jet. She could tell that he knew exactly who'd been on the phone.

"You have to go," he said.

"I do." She swallowed, reminded herself that he was her boss. "Is that okay?"

"Of course."

She would be okay, she sternly told herself. She'd survived worse, and really, what was the worst that could happen? If her daughter had a disease, they'd deal with it, but the odds were in her favor that nothing was seriously wrong.

"Thanks." She reminded herself to breathe. "If you wouldn't mind sharing with your sister why I had to leave, I'd appreciate it. Tell her I'm sorry."

"She'll understand."

She grabbed her purse from her drawer, but her hands shook so badly she dropped it the moment she stood. She picked it up, the resulting head rush causing her to sway.

"Are you okay?"

No. I'm not okay. I'm terrified for my kid.

"Fine."

He frowned. She ignored him, took another deep breath and made her way around her desk. He stood, too, but as she brushed past him, she felt his hand at the small of her back. "Let me see you out."

"That's not necessary."

"Just the same, I'm going to do it."

She stopped. "No."

"Oh, for goodness' sake." He shook his head. "Will you stop acting like Superwoman? You don't have to do this alone, you know. You have friends."

"I don't feel alone."

But she lied. She felt like the only person in the world

right then. She tried—Lord, how she tried—to hide it from him, but it felt as though he could see into her soul.

"Come on," he said, guiding her toward the door once again.

She let him. They passed the Baron Energies receptionist again, Jet saying, "Be right back." She even allowed him to push the poor, pummeled button for her at the elevator, and all the while her heart pounded and pounded and pounded.

Don't panic.

She recognized the symptoms, though. She'd had a bout with anxiety right after Darren had died. She'd told herself it was hormones. Newly pregnant. Fiancé dead. Who wouldn't have an attack or two? Yet here she was, four years later, her chest contracting and expanding with greater and greater frequency. Her peripheral vision fading around the edges. Sound seemed to recede until all she heard was a rushing in her ears. She knew, she just knew, if she didn't get control soon, she'd lose it entirely. When the elevator announced its arrival with a *ding,* she jumped.

"Easy, there."

He helped guide her into the elevator. She blinked with more and more frequency.

Get it together.

By God, she would. She hadn't grown up the daughter of a roughneck for nothing.

She'll be fine, Jasmine.

Eyes she hadn't even known she'd closed popped open again. Her dad's voice. She hadn't heard it in years. Not since…Darren.

Deep breath.

Was that her subconscious? Or her dad's voice again? The elevator began to drop. When she glanced up she saw that Jet had stayed with her. He stared down at her in concern. That, more than anything, caused her to tip her chin up and say, "I'm fine. I'll be fine."

"I know." He smiled. "You have the strength of a mountain lion. It's something I really admire about you, but I'm going with you."

His words had left her so flummoxed, she didn't know what to say...so she said nothing at all.

Chapter Eleven

They emerged from the elevator, and Jet could tell by her body language her Superwoman routine was all an act. He kept glancing at her as they made their way across the lobby's marble floor, a tall bank of windows allowing sunlight to warm the air. They passed potted palms that smelled musty, as if they'd been recently watered, and another bank of elevators and other people in suits and jackets and even jeans like himself. She didn't say a word as they exited, but when he spotted her familiar silver truck parked between two smaller cars in Baron's underground parking lot, he held out his hand.

"Keys."

She shook her head. "I can manage."

He turned, grabbed her by the shoulders, wondered briefly what it was about her that made him want to pull her toward him and hold her, even when another part warned him away. Even now he had to fight the urge to do exactly that.

"Listen, when my sister had her pregnancy health scare, she had someone with her the whole time. My other sister, too. She had her future fiancé with her when she thought she had a lump in her breast. My point being there are times in one's life when having a friend around is a good thing, and so I'm going with you. Deal with it."

He strode to her truck and stood by the driver's door. "Keys."

He wasn't sure what to make of the expression on her face. Was that gratitude? Resignation? Or just plain irritation? Perhaps all of the above, but in the end, she reached into her purse, fished for the keys, then handed them to him. He wasted no time in placing a hand on the small of her back and guiding her into the passenger seat of her vehicle.

"Buckle up."

He didn't give her time to answer, just jogged around to the other side, his mind going a hundred miles per hour. What if one of his sisters went through something similar? What if his soon-to-be-born nephew or niece became ill? Gosh. Just thinking about it caused his heart to beat hard and his stomach to turn—and it wasn't even a real-time scenario. How much worse must Jasmine feel?

He was doing the right thing, he thought, having to wedge himself between the steering wheel and her seat. He might not be a father, might not ever be father material, but that didn't mean he didn't care.

She was shorter than him. Not by much, but enough that he had to fix the mirrors and the seat before he backed out of the spot. His sister might not approve. Hell, his sister might just tell him to forget about working for Baron Energies, but he knew in his heart he was making the right move.

Jasmine gave him directions. They headed toward the outskirts of downtown. Brooke's doctor was in a nondescript, two-story brown building that housed a million other doctors judging by the sign out front. They escaped the humid Texas heat, entering a main lobby area with a stairwell and a set of elevators and numerous doors set at odd intervals. Her doctor's name—a Dr. Lee— was written on a piece of Plexiglas in a block print. He heard her take a deep breath before pushing on the door.

"Go ahead and take a seat. I'll tell them you're here."

He thought she might protest, thought she might flip on the I'm-just-fine switch, but she didn't. Damn. He felt as nervous as an expectant father.

He would have known they stood in a pediatrician's office without having seen the doctor's credentials on the door. The place had walls painted in a rainbow of colors. A play area sat to their left. A TV to their right played a popular Disney movie. Nobody was there, though, the place oddly deserted. Maybe that was a good thing. He still wasn't comfortable with the whole kid thing. He headed straight for a counter with a window across the top. An attractive brunette opened the sliding glass.

"Can I help you?"

"Jasmine Marks is here to see Dr. Lee."

The woman nodded. She turned to another woman sitting next to her, an older, gray-haired nurse judging by the scrubs she wore. That woman looked up, met his gaze and smiled professionally.

"Come on back," said the nurse.

Jasmine must have heard because he didn't even have time to call her over. Suddenly, she was right there. They both slipped through a door to the right of the reception area and followed the nurse down a short hallway.

He thought they'd be led to an exam room. Instead, they were led to the doctor's private office, the man standing up behind a massive oak desk the moment they entered. He'd been waiting for them. Jet wasn't sure what to make of that, but he knew if he was thinking dire thoughts, Jasmine would be, too. Twentyfold.

"Sit down, please," said Dr. Lee.

He seemed young for a doctor, but Jet could see why Jasmine had brought her girls to him. He had kind brown eyes and a soft smile that undoubtedly set children at ease. When Jet took a seat in an armchair in front of the doctor's desk, he was surprised to feel Jasmine's hand seek out his own. Her cold fingers slid through his.

"I'm glad you could make it in this morning," the doctor began without preamble. "I'm sure you've surmised that I wouldn't have asked you here unless I was concerned about the results of Brooke's blood work."

Out of the corner of his eye, he saw Jasmine nod. The doctor turned to him next. "Are you Brooke's father?"

"No," he said quickly. "I'm Jasmine's friend." He forced his own smile. "I'm here for moral support."

"I see." The doctor caught Jasmine's gaze, held it a moment before saying, "As you know, we were looking for the presence of a virus in Brooke's blood." He slid a paper toward Jasmine who leaned forward and took it. The word NEGATIVE was emblazoned under a column labeled RESULTS.

"Honestly, I fully expected she had the latest rhinovirus going around, but that's not the case at all, which means there has to be another problem."

Jet knew all Jasmine heard was the word *problem*. She hid it well, but her hand began to squeeze his own.

"What do we do next?" Her voice cracked and it broke Jet's heart. He knew that deep inside she must be completely panicked.

"Unfortunately, more blood work. We'll need to focus on certain areas of concern. This weekend we didn't have her fast before drawing blood because I was just doing a simple virus check. This time we'll do a full blood panel plus take a urine sample and do a more thorough exam. I'll be looking for lumps and unusual bruising."

"She doesn't have any of those."

"I'm glad to hear it," Dr. Lee said. "But sometimes they can be hard to spot. I'll want to see her right away, if that's okay. If you could bring her back this evening, that would be ideal, but make sure she has nothing to eat or drink for the rest of the day. My office will be closed and so it would be an ideal time in the event we have some…difficulties drawing blood or during the exam. You know how kids are. It can be uncomfortable for the most easy of children."

Meaning he didn't want Brooke upsetting his patients. Jet understood what the man was getting at even if he didn't come right out and say it.

"Of course," Jasmine said. "I'll just have to clear it with work."

"Don't worry about that," Jet said. "My sister will understand."

"Very well," the doctor said. "I'll see you at four this afternoon, then."

She held it together while saying goodbye to the doctor and his staff. She held it together as they made their way across the lobby and then to her truck. She lasted until she climbed inside and he closed the door. Then and only then, when he was out of earshot, on the other side of a closed door, did she lose control, although not completely. He saw her face crumble and her lips tremble, but she didn't cry.

She might as well have.

Her fear and distress and sadness were all there—every line on her face painted the picture, one of despair. He wanted to open the door again, to pull her into his arms, but something stopped him. Instead, he pretended as if he didn't see it, just made his way to the other side, feeling as miserable as she looked.

"Where to?" he asked because, if he were honest, he didn't know what to say. Telling her that everything would be all right seemed too trite.

"Office."

"No."

She glanced at him sharply. Still no tears.

"I'm taking you home."

"Don't do that."

"You have no choice. I'm going to call my sister and tell her what's going on and that you need to be at home with your little girl right now. No, no. Don't say a word. You're going home, if for no other reason than to give your daughter a hug, okay?"

Oddly, his words seemed to pull a tear from her eye. "You don't need to do that."

"Just the same, I am."

HE WAS RIGHT.

She was in no condition to work. She could barely keep breathing without crying, much less make polite conversation.

Relax, Jasmine, it's probably nothing.

But life had frequently given her lemons and unlike most people, it very rarely resulted in lemonade. She had to be realistic. That was just the way she was programmed these days. The thought of trying to sit through the rest of the day, all the while worrying and wondering and waiting for four o'clock to roll around… Better to go home now, as he said. Home, where she could hold Brooke and close her eyes and pretend as if they lived in a world where children never grew ill and medicine wasn't needed.

A hand fell over her own. She almost jumped.

"It'll be okay." He gave her a reassuring smile before starting the engine.

They drove in silence. She had no idea how he knew where she lived, and was about to ask before realizing he followed the GPS she had on her dash. At some point he must have pressed the home button. She hadn't even noticed. He didn't know her unit number, though, so she pointed the way, her voice as shaky as an old lady's when she said, "Park there."

"Looks like a nice place."

"It is." She popped the door open before he could say another word, so anxious to see Brooke—as if something might happen if she didn't rush to see her—that when she went to slam the door closed, the thing didn't shut all the way. Seat belt. The metal piece had wedged itself in the jam. She turned back to fix it.

"It's okay. I'll get it."

He'd hopped out of the truck, too, and it was then that she had another thought.

"How will you get home?" She flicked the seat belt out of the way, the retractor whizzing back into place. She slammed the door.

"I've asked Lizzie to come get me."

He kept moving forward, and she wondered why for a moment before she realized he held out her keys, which she took. "Your sister? You didn't have to do that. I feel bad enough as it is. I'll call you a cab or something."

"I already sent her a text message." He took her by the shoulder and turned her toward the sidewalk. "Go."

She felt as dazed as a bombing victim. "When did you text her?"

"While I was at a stoplight."

She'd been so busy trying to keep her emotions under

wraps she hadn't even noticed. Even now she had to fight to keep her hands from trembling as she allowed him to guide her forward.

"Which one is yours?"

"Bottom floor. First one on the left." Her feet moved by rote down the concrete path. Weeks ago she'd fallen in love with the multistory complex with its lush landscape and steep roofs. Each unit came with its own balcony trimmed in wood. The facades were brick and there was enough spacing between the buildings that it didn't feel as if she could pass the mustard to her neighbor if she opened a window.

"Is this it?"

She looked up. They stood before a door, one that suddenly felt as terrifying as the opening of a cave, and she knew, she just knew that once she opened that door her pretense at calm would be at an end.

She spun to face him. "Thank you for bringing me here."

He nodded. "Of course."

"I'll see you tomorrow."

"Not if your daughter needs you."

She nodded sharply. "I will, I mean, I can't exactly drop everything just because my child is ill."

He gently cupped her chin. She'd had no idea he'd moved so close. "Yes, you can."

She had no idea how close she was to tears until she looked into his eyes, looked into them and saw kindness and gentleness and sympathetic understanding.

"I'll let you know."

His fingers stroked the side of her face, and he appeared troubled and torn and bothered by the sight of her tears. She knew it was wrong of her, that she shouldn't have thoughts about how handsome he was, not now.

TEC

Yet those were exactly the thoughts running through her head. Something fluttered through her, something unexpected and terrifying.

"It'll be all right," he said, and when he bent down, when his lips began to lower, she didn't move, couldn't move. "I know it'll all work out."

Softness brushed her lips, a butterfly wing's touch, a caress of kindness and concern and caring. Then it was gone.

"I'll call you tomorrow."

And then he was gone.

Chapter Twelve

"I'm not going to say a word."

Jet lifted his hands in a praise of the Lord.

"I mean, it's not like we haven't discussed your involvement with our new engineer before. You know my feelings on the matter."

His sister could be a real pain in the rear sometimes, Jet thought, propping his feet up on the dash of her company Mercedes. "If you'd seen her at the office you'd have offered to drive her there, too."

"Get your feet down." She slapped his legs. They dropped to the floor.

"Hey."

"I swear, Jet, sometimes you act six years old."

"It's a company car."

"Yes, and when we ferry around big wigs, the last thing I want them to see are scuff marks on the dash."

"You're just angry because you had to pick me up."

"There's that, too." She glanced at him as she pulled out of Jasmine's apartment complex. "Some of us actually work for a living."

"Like I don't."

"Not today, you didn't."

"Come on. I've been pulling my weight. We're digging the footings for the rig this week."

"You should have been digging them last week."

He shook his head. "Man, you really are a slave driver."

"No, no, no." She shook her own head, only more emphatically. "I am an employee of Baron Energies."

He glanced over at her, his eyes sliding past her profile and catching on the neighboring apartment buildings, and beyond that, the Dallas skyline. "Like I'm not?"

She didn't answer immediately, but that was okay. She was driving and, in his opinion, his sister had never been very good at talking and driving at the same time.

"We're under a microscope, you and I. If it's not Dad looking over our shoulders, it's a member of the board of directors, and I have to be honest, if the board catches wind of your little friendship with our new engineer, I don't think they'd be happy. They're already up in arms about the whole AB Windpower thing."

What was this? "What AB Windpower thing?"

Lizzie shrugged. "It's nothing."

"Clearly it's something if you're bringing it up now."

She shook in her head.

"Something I should be worried about?"

"No," she said firmly. "Just a little stock activity that we've yet to get to the bottom of. It's no big deal. It's not like a corporate takeover or anything, it's just… bothersome."

"Sounds like you have more to worry about than me."

"You're just the icing on the cake. I live in fear of the next lawsuit."

"Jasmine would never do something like that."

"So you've indicated, but do you really know her well enough to judge that?"

Yes, he did, but he didn't see the point in arguing and

so he said nothing at all, at least not until he glanced at his sister again and saw her rubbing her belly. She'd be giving birth soon.

"How would you feel if your child was ill?"

She glanced at him sharply.

"If there was nobody to hold your hand while you went through it all?" He felt his own stomach flip, something from the edges coalescing into warmth and making him feel...different inside. "If you didn't have Chris standing by your side."

They cruised to a stop at a light, just in time, too. "All right, all right." She lifted a hand off the wheel, her blue eyes flashing.

"I was just trying to be a friend."

But that got her shaking her head again. "You like this woman, Jet. Admit it."

He opened his mouth to deny it, but what was the use? "I do, but I'm not a fool. Even I know a relationship with her would be fraught with difficulties, and not just because of the work thing. I understand what it means to take on the responsibility of two kids."

She was staring at him intently. "Wow. I really think you do."

"I do. Believe me. It's been keeping me awake at night."

"I know how that feels."

"Is that how it was with you and Chris?"

"Yup, although it took me a while to admit I had feelings for him."

That's where he was at, too. Did he throw in the towel? Or continue to keep Jasmine at arm's length. He almost snorted. Arm's length. Like he'd been doing that lately.

"She's going to need a friend."

"When have you ever been able to be just a friend to a woman?"

He knew the answer. Never. He loved female companionship, but if he were honest with himself, that's all it really was—companionship. He'd never taken any woman he'd dated seriously, and yet here he was, contemplating what it would be like to date someone with two little girls, one of whom might be sick.

It should scare the hell out of him. For some reason, it didn't.

THE DOCTOR'S VISIT was not pleasant.

Brooke screamed practically the entire time. Blood work, urine samples, a physical exam that included poking and prodding and the coldness of a stethoscope pressed to her body. Her poor child didn't understand, and it broke Jasmine's heart to hear her cry, "Mommy, Mommy, Mommy," as if she would make it all stop.

By the time they returned home later that evening, Jasmine was near tears herself. Somehow she managed to cook dinner without burning it—fried chicken, the girls' favorite—and then get them in the bath and then bed. She changed into a T-shirt and sweats, brushed out her own hair, and waited for exhaustion to overcome her. It didn't. She was too tense, too filled with worry, too... scared, so she settled on her couch, resting her head on the back of it and wishing...wishing. She bit her lip. Just wishing her baby would be okay.

Her phone chimed. She hadn't even remembered grabbing it. She glanced at the coffee table in front of her. Text message, but when she saw who it was from, she didn't know what to think.

You okay? Jet had typed.

She frowned, shook her head. *Don't answer. Do* not *answer.*

Yes, she found herself typing. Why did her heart pound while she waited for a reply?

Kids in bed?

Yes.

Going to bed?

She sighed, wondering if he'd meant the words to sound suggestive, before admitting he probably didn't.

Not for a while. Too keyed up.

If I tell you something will you promise not to get mad?

She frowned, wondering what he needed to tell her, only to jerk upright. Crud. What if she'd been fired? What if his sister had blown up at him for taking her to the doctor? What if she had no job?

What?

She waited, heart pounding. Of course, he took his time responding. She began to fret even more until the chime of a text made her jump.

I'm outside your apartment.

She nearly dropped the phone. Not ten seconds later he knocked on the door. She glanced at the kids' bedroom, wondering if it would wake them up, and if the first knock hadn't woken them up, if another knock would.

"Crap." She jumped up, and when she opened the door, his smile said it all.

Surprise.

For about 3.9 seconds she thought about slamming the door in his face. One thing stopped her. She was glad to see him. She couldn't deny it, had to wrestle her conscience to the ground before she could admit it, but she gave in to the urge to smile at him nonetheless, albeit a small smile and one tinged with admonition.

He held up a bottle of wine. She almost closed her eyes and said a prayer in thanks, but behind her eyelids the image of him still burned bright. White button-down, starched jeans, black hair mussed—as if he'd been wearing a cowboy hat earlier and hadn't bothered to brush it out. *Gorgeous.*

She moved before the thought could complicate matters. "Come on in."

He beamed. "If I'd known all it would take was a bottle of wine, I'd have tried that days ago."

"A few days ago not even a bottle of whiskey would have gotten you in."

How strange to think that a few weeks ago she hadn't even known him. Now here she was, motioning toward her couch, but not before holding her hand out for the bottle of wine, then heading to her kitchen in search of a bottle opener. She heard the couch sigh as he took a seat. A moment later she joined him, two glasses of wine in hand, bubbles gathering around the line of liquid. He moved some pillows aside so she could sit. The wine, whatever it was, smelled sweet, faintly fruity.

"My sister made it. Not Lizzie, but Savannah. Strawberry wine. She's always trying to think of something new to sell at her store."

Strawberry wine? She took a hesitant sip, feeling her brows lift in surprise. "It's good."

He smiled, but it faded quickly. "Was it really bad?"

It took a few seconds to understand his meaning, but when she did, she immediately looked away from his intense stare. The memory of Brooke screaming left her feeling ill.

"Bad enough."

"Did they discover anything?"

"Nothing obvious. He poked and prodded and squeezed and probed until she screamed herself hoarse. He said the good news was nothing appears to be obviously wrong. Her kidneys felt normal and no swollen glands that he could tell. He took more blood, checked her for bruising, so right now it's just wait and see if something shows up in her blood panel, and maybe a CAT scan."

To look for tumors. She closed her eyes, taking a quick sip of the wine. Goodness, she didn't want to think about that. If her daughter had—

She couldn't even *think* the *C* word.

A hand landed on her shoulder. She nearly jumped again. Thankfully, she didn't, her gaze locking on his own, the same kindness and concern she'd spotted earlier. The memory of his kiss—that butterfly's kiss—made her cheeks fill with color and her insides to flutter like wings. He took her glass from her. She let him. She heard rather than saw him set it down. Her gaze had grown unfocused as she tried to analyze every riotous emotion bouncing around inside of her.

"Jasmine." His voice was soft, a verbal caress of gentleness, and she knew what he wanted to do before he slowly pulled her into his arms. He didn't try to kiss her, not at first, and she appreciated his restraint because she longed to be held, longed to be soothed, wanted to hear everything would be all right, and in his touch, she found the comfort she needed.

"It's okay."

She closed her eyes as warmth from his body seemed to heat her own chilled soul. Somehow, she ended up on his lap in a childlike position that made her sigh even as a part of her wondered what he wanted from her and where they were going with whatever this was between them.

Don't think.

She heeded her own advice, emptying her mind, absorbing his strength, the feel of his big arms around her soothing her in a way she hadn't been soothed in years.

"You'll see." His voice rumbled beneath her ear. His chin rested on the top of her head. "Everything will be fine."

He stroked her head and she admitted this was exactly what she needed. Companionship. Support. *A friend.*

She leaned back, caught his eye.

And it changed.

Just like that. In the blink of an eye. She went from content to combustible. He did, too. The heat of his own gaze lit up like the surface of the sun. When his head began to drift toward her own, she closed her eyes once again, but for a whole other reason. She felt his breath on her first, then the soft brush of his mouth, and the moment his lips touched her own, she remembered that she was a flesh-and-blood woman, one who hadn't been with a man in a long, long time.

Her mouth opened.

The gentle touch of his tongue had her remembering

what it was like to be with a man. She released a keening
mew of longing. The taste of him—wine and strawberries—did something to her, dislodged something she'd
forgotten about during those long, lonely nights. Desire.
Lust. Need. It pooled in her abdomen only to spiral out-
ward, igniting nerve endings along the way.

His hand lowered. She felt his fingers skate down her
neck, leaving goose bumps in their wake, then across
the top of her left shoulder, sliding downward and toward the slope of her breast. She gasped.

He'd touched her.

And not even bare flesh. She wore no bra, but she
may as well have not worn anything. Just the weight of
his hand was enough to make her change the angle of
her head, to kiss him harder and deeper. The pressure
on her breast grew. She arched into it. His palm found
the soft tip of her breast, his fingers kneaded the sides,
lifted it, his lips slowly withdrawing from her own and
skimming ever so slowly down the line of her jaw until
he found the cords of her neck. Lord help her, she hadn't
felt the soft nips of a man's mouth in so long she couldn't
stop the groan that rose up from deep inside. She felt
the sweet suckle of his mouth and the sparks she saw
ignited her whole body.

He was all hard male against her, and when their
gazes connected, his eyes silently asked a question.

Should I stop?

Yes. No. She didn't know. All she knew was that for
the first time in a long, long while she felt like a woman,
not the single mother of two or a woman trying to hold
it all together or someone pretending to be a good mom
when deep inside she felt anything but.

Her eyes must have given him an answer, for his head
lowered, and she realized she needed this…this…what-

ever it was. She needed it desperately. Because also for the first time in a long, long while, she didn't feel alone.

"Bedroom is that way." She pointed left.

He smiled.

Chapter Thirteen

She trembled, and his heart melted.

Jet set her down.

It'd been a long time for her, he realized. And so even though all he wanted to do was jerk the T-shirt and sweats off her body, instead, he paused for a moment. Her head lay against the pillow, her eyes as blue as a butterfly wing. She stared up at him, so extraordinarily beautiful with her blond hair around her head and her lips red from his kisses all he wanted to do was stare. She had no idea how stunning she was, he thought. She was too busy trying to prove to the world that she could do it all with her two kids and fancy degree.

Don't think about the two kids.

He'd worry about that later. For now he touched a lock of hair next to her cheek. He meant to finger it, to test the softness of it between his thumb and forefinger. Instead, he touched her cheek. Her eyes closed, her lips releasing a sigh. Skin so smooth it felt as if he stroked baby-fine hairs. He touched her nose next. So small. And then her lips. So full, and just as soft as her cheek.

He kissed her.

She tasted of strawberries and the tannin in the wine and when she opened her mouth the gossamer thread of control that held him back suddenly ignited like a fuse.

He couldn't believe the effect she had on him. She made him want things. God help him, she made him think about white picket fences and twin girls playing outside.

Their hands found each other. Fingers entwined. She lifted her arms, and he realized what she silently asked him to do. He wasted no time, pulling the shirt from her body in one fluid motion and in the process, revealing her breasts. He leaned in and tasted one. She arched into him, and he marveled that this part of her body, too, could be so soft and warm.

"Jet." She sighed.

His released the hardened nub and began to taste the valley between her breasts. He followed the dent of her sternum with his tongue, finding her belly button and then her abdomen, flirting with the line of flesh above her waistline. He tipped the fabric lower. She moaned.

"Shh," he soothed.

He suckled, swirling his tongue around and around, nipping at times, her moans of pleasure heightening his anticipation and causing him to tremble. His hand lowered. His palm slid beneath the fabric of her sweats and found her center, and she released a cry of pleasure.

"Shh," he warned again, worrying about waking the girls. It disconcerted him to think about the two children sleeping a few feet away. For a moment he wondered if he should stop. Lord, he'd never been with a woman with kids before. What if one of them came in?

He was about to pull back when she ran her hand through his hair. Their gazes locked. She'd left the light on in her bathroom and so he could perfectly see the sizzle in her deep blue eyes.

He forgot about the children.

She sat up. He did, too, his whole body tensing as she reached for his waistband. Her hands brushed him as she popped the snap of his jeans. It was his turn to close his eyes. He heard his zipper lower. When he felt her hand return to grasp him, he almost groaned. He kissed her again, and she returned the favor—their hands went to work, and this time he couldn't contain a groan. He leaned back, and she followed him down, arching into him, and he kissed her harder, his tongue swiping deep into her mouth in the same rhythm as his hand.

They had to slow down.

A part of him knew that. He'd lose it if they kept this up much longer and it left him feeling awed that she could arouse him so quickly and completely. Still, he drew back.

"You're going to kill me," he gasped.

"Don't stop." She sounded as if she'd run a marathon. Her fingers began to work the buttons on his shirt. His own fingers tugged down the waistline of her sweats. Suddenly, they both began to move quickly. She slid his shirt over his shoulders. Her sweats were flung off to the side. His jeans were discarded. His fingers found her undies. She found his. It was as if having committed to the course they were both impatient, but when she slid his Jockey shorts down....

He hissed.

Her hand grazed him. She must have caught his reaction because she clasped him next and he just about exploded.

He went back to kissing her again. Skin met skin. Her sweet taste, the way she boldly touched him—all of it was like nothing he'd ever experienced before.

He drew back for breath. "We should slow down."

"I don't want it slow."

"Jasmine—"

"I want it *now.*"

"We need protection."

"Nightstand."

Nightstand?

She must have seen the consternation he felt upon learning she kept condoms near her bed.

"I found them during the move. They've been in there for a while."

Jealous. He had no right to be. He'd certainly been no monk himself, and yet the thought of her being with another man… Completely irrational. This whole thing didn't make sense. He hated commitment and yet he knew that with a woman like Jasmine, that's what he faced.

She grabbed his hand, kissed it, as if sensing his doubts that they were doing the right thing, and the simple touch had him turning toward the nightstand. She helped him pull on protection, and the feel of her soft fingers had him closing his eyes all over again. Lord have mercy, she'd be the death of him at this rate.

He felt rather than saw her shift and he knew she was lying down. She found his hand, pulled him on top of her, and her eagerness aroused him all the more. He told himself to take it slow but he couldn't seem to stop himself. He didn't want to take his time, either. She bucked her hips when he drew near. He slipped between her thighs. When he found her center they both gasped. Jet bent to kiss her again but as he lowered his head he froze when he saw the look in her eyes.

Satisfaction.

Like a cat stretching after a long nap, she seemed utterly content. The look tipped his world on its axis. Up was down and down was up. Something inside him shifted, too.

He *wanted* to please her. Wanted to please her so

badly it was an ache in his gut and it threw him for a loop, this…this *need* to satisfy her.

He didn't kiss her. Instead, he held her hands as he watched the play of emotion in her eyes. She watched him, too. He moved. Withdrew. Moved again. Her grip grew tighter and tighter. The contentment faded. Heat took its place. Her grip tightened even more. And as they climbed higher and higher, it felt as if Jet waited, although he didn't know what for. Her hips jerked. He gasped. Her whole body clutched him, tighter and tighter, her eyes growing darker and darker until suddenly she cried out, her lashes sweeping down, her head tipping back and he knew she'd found her release. He found his, too, and yet he never looked away, never stopped watching her, reveled in how completely she lost control.

That was how, a few moments later, he spotted her tears.

"What?" he asked gently.

Her eyes opened, pupils flaring, light blue returning. "Nothing."

But he knew that wasn't true. "Did I hurt you?"

She shook her head.

"What is it?" he asked, sliding a hand against her cheek.

"It's just…" She blinked a few times. "I haven't been with anyone other than Darren and I didn't think it would be… I wasn't sure I would…"

"Enjoy yourself?"

And suddenly she seemed shy. And it made his heart melt all over again. No one else other than Darren? How could that be?

He bent to kiss her, whispering against her lips, "There's more where that came from."

SHE AWOKE TO the sound of Brooke crying. It made her sit up and instantly throw the covers back.

She was naked.

A quick glance at the bed revealed Jet still sound asleep, a sheet wound around his middle, his handsome face softened by the light in her bathroom and the peacefulness of satiation. She felt instantly self-conscious for some silly reason, but she had no time to fret about it. She snatched up her sweats and shirt, all the while wondering what the heck she'd been thinking to fall asleep in his arms. Had they even locked the door?

They hadn't.

She was down the hall and in Brooke and Gwen's room in a flash. Her daughter had kicked off the covers on her bed. Blue eyes were wide-open, lids rimmed by red, her face a frown of discomfort. Gwen, however, seemed impervious to it all. She lay on her own bed, sound asleep.

"What is it, baby?" she asked softly.

"Mommy."

Her precious baby girl held out her arms. When she lifted her up, Jasmine could see why she cried. A wet spot stood out like a blotch of ink on parchment paper. She'd been doing that a lot lately. Whole body sweats. Her poor little girl woke up wringing wet and miserable and soon she would know why. Very soon.

"Shh," she soothed, though her heart had begun to beat in fear. The peace she'd found in Jet's arms faded to nothing. "It's okay. Let's get you changed."

Brooke still snuffled, her head resting on her shoulder as Jasmine somehow managed to juggle her daughter, the dresser drawer and a new set of pajamas. When she'd finished up, she scooped her daughter back up in her arms and cuddled her in a chair near the dresser, all the while trying to figure out the best way to change the sheets.

"Is everything all right?"

She jumped at the sound of the masculine voice. Gwen was out cold, and Brooke appeared to have fallen back to sleep again.

His gaze swept the room, landing on Brooke in her arms, but shifted to the bed. She saw it then, the instant flash of trepidation. "Do you need help?"

He'd dressed, thankfully, and he forced a smile. She supposed it should reassure her, really, that Jet seemed to grasp the seriousness of dealing with children. It would take some adjustment on his part, but he didn't leave. Seeing him there, all broad shoulders and tall masculinity, created a feeling within her that she couldn't deny, and that scared her to pieces.

"It's okay. I've got it."

She slowly stood, trying to sneak a glance at her daughter to see if she'd woken her, but couldn't from the angle she was at. Didn't matter.

"Thanks, though," she said, trying to smile, sliding past him and heading toward the hall closet.

The cabinet that held her linens was just outside her room, but as she tried to juggle her child and the cabinet door she felt Brooke slide down one shoulder. She shifted her back into place, but Jet took matters into his own hand.

"What do you need?" When she looked into his eyes she could see determination there.

Inwardly, she sighed in relief. "Sheets for a toddler bed." She kept her voice low. "There on the right."

"Got it. You sit down."

She was about to tell him she could do it, but that was just plain silly. So she settled herself in the rocking chair again. Brooke snuggled even closer when she felt the familiar position. How many times had she rocked her child to sleep? Brooke was such a cuddle-monkey, the child that had needed her mother's arms. Right now her hair was matted with sweat, though the edges had dried and curled like angel feathers. She nuzzled those strands and began to rock.

How long she sat there, she didn't know. Long enough that she knew Brooke was well and truly asleep. When she looked up, Jet stared at her. He'd sat on the bed although she couldn't remember him doing it. He just watched, and for some reason it made her feel even more self-conscious. When she stood, he got up, too, pulling the pink Disney Princess covers back and then fluffing the pillow. Her sweet little girl clung to her on the way down, but when she felt the bed beneath her she burrowed beneath the covers and as Jasmine caught a glimpse of her pale face, fear filled her once more.

"She'll be okay."

She nodded.

"I promise you, Jasmine. It'll all work out."

She took a breath, then met his gaze. She could get used to this, the pep talks at midnight, used to having him by her side. But in reality she doubted she would ever let him near her again. She prided herself on her honesty, and if she were honest, she could admit to using him right now. She hated it. Didn't like thinking about how selfish it was, but it was true. She'd needed a warm body tonight and so she'd taken him. She didn't delude herself that this was some kind of long-term romance. He would be glad for the escape, too, she told herself. Children made him uncomfortable. She could see that, but Brooke and Gwen were asleep now and she wasn't ready to let him go. Not yet.

"Thanks," she said.

He watched her. She wanted him to kiss her again. No. She needed him to do that. She needed to forget for a few more minutes all that she would have to face in the coming days.

So she took his hand.

He let her lead him away, and she was grateful because this was what she wanted. At least for a little while. By morning he would have to go. She didn't need questions from her daughters. She hoped Brooke had been out of it enough that she wouldn't remember seeing the man in her room.

She led him to her bedroom, and for a little while she did forget, and in the morning he seemed to understand her need to have him leave. She was grateful for that, but as she kissed him goodbye, something that felt close to tears warmed her eyes. Stupid. She had no need for tears. She'd known what she was getting into, and it wasn't a long-term relationship with Jet.

"Thanks for everything."

There was something in his eyes as she kissed him goodbye, something that troubled her and made her catch her breath.

"I'll see you at work," he said.

Yes, work, because this could go no further than the one night. He knew that, and she did, too.

"Drive carefully."

Steeling herself against all the doubts and uncertainty that swirled through her insides she closed the door, reminding herself that the last thing she needed right now was a man in the picture, one who would make her girls fall in love with him, and then leave, or worse, die riding some stupid bull. She'd been down that road and she would never put herself in that position again. She would never put the girls in the position of caring for someone only to have him ripped away…for whatever reason.

Not ever.

Chapter Fourteen

Jet tried to keep the panic at bay.

He'd screwed up. He'd let things get out of hand with Jasmine. Lizzie would take one look at his face and know what had happened. Maybe that's how she'd figured out he'd been the one to let the cattle out, and when he'd been older, the one who'd chopped off one of Carly's braids. How the hell would he keep what had happened with Jasmine a secret?

Why did he want to?

He rested his head in his hands. She'd kissed him goodbye. Sent him on his way. That was good. She hadn't demanded to see him again. She had no idea he'd had a momentary flash of panic at the thought that she might. And then there was her daughter. Her sick kid. He'd felt so helpless last night. Was that what being a parent felt like? Helpless and scared and worried? He'd never really been scared of anything in his life, not even a fifteen-hundred-pound bull. He had to admit, he didn't like it.

"You look mighty glum."

He jumped. Lord, his sister was like an evil spirit. One thought and she materialized like a jinni in front of you. He had to fight to paste a smile on his face, but he must not have done a good job.

"What's wrong?"

"Nothing," he said quickly. "I was just thinking about your search for Mom."

It wasn't exactly a lie. He'd had the thought this morning as he'd driven away from Jasmine's house that that's exactly what his own mother had done. Driven away. He wasn't even close to Jasmine's kids, not by a long shot, but even with all that was going on between him and Jasmine, he still found it hard to fathom, couldn't imagine someone like Jasmine leaving her kids. Not ever.

"I've been thinking about her, too."

She touched her belly as she took a seat. She looked good for a pregnant woman in her dark blue dress. She should look fat. Wasn't that how it worked? But his sister had always been pretty, and pregnancy suited her, especially when she tucked her hair into a bun.

"And I realized I was being something of a hypocrite."

That had him straightening up. "Oh, yeah?"

She nodded. "Mom left us and being pregnant has made me wonder why. I get angry when I think about what she did. Angry and frustrated and, yes, hurt."

He'd never given their mother a thought, not until he'd met Jasmine, and suddenly he felt the same way.

"So here I am angry that she left us, and there I was yesterday telling you to leave Jasmine alone at a time when she needs you the most." She frowned. "Hypocrite."

His sister appeared so genuinely torn, so completely contrite that Jet felt his heart soften with love. He could always count on Lizzie to give it to him straight, even when the tables were turned and she felt that she was in the wrong.

"Anyway, I understand why you helped. I don't like it. I worry she might get the wrong idea, but I understand."

He felt his neck begin to flush. Damn it. He hoped she didn't see, tried to distract her by saying, "Thanks for understanding," and then pasting a big smile on his face. "And hey, I've got some good news. I had a voice mail this morning. Our new road is almost finished, our reserve pits are dug, the footings are going in today, we're ready to start drilling for water and, once we have that, the good kind of drilling begins."

She'd spotted the flush. He could tell. Her eyes had slowly narrowed while he'd given his speech. "What's going on?"

He gulped. A pile of paper on his desk caught his attention. He pretended to thumb through it.

"Nothing. Nothing at all."

"You were with her last night, weren't you?"

He set the papers down. "Lizzie, where I was last night is none of your concern. As you so aptly pointed out to me yesterday, I am an employee of Baron Energies. My personal life is none of your concern, boss lady." *Actually, it should be* bossy *lady.* "Plus, I'm a grown man. I can take care of myself."

"Oh, I know you can take care of yourself. My concern is your ability to safeguard this company."

"So you've mentioned."

"I mean it, Jet. I spoke to J.C. this morning. Told her to take a few days off, but now I'm glad I did for a different reason. You are seriously messing with corporate fire."

He glanced up sharply. "I've got it under control."

"Hah. Famous last words. She's...vulnerable right now. And she has two little girls, one of whom might be seriously ill. It's easy to confuse lust for love, and if you hurt J.C., you'll end up hurting those two little girls, too, and maybe even this company if she's the spurned-lover type of woman who'd file a lawsuit out of spite."

"She wouldn't do that."

"Let's hope not."

She stood abruptly, clearly upset, and Jet didn't blame her. He might not take certain things seriously, but he understood his sister's concerns. He felt the same concern himself.

"I'm not an idiot," he called out after her, but the words were more to reassure himself than his sister. He wasn't going to hurt anybody. And Jasmine wasn't going to sue Baron Energies.

But his sister's words haunted him for the rest of the day. He didn't hear from Jasmine and he told himself that was good. Space. That's what they needed. Still, he almost picked up the phone at least a half a dozen times. He was genuinely concerned for Brooke. He wanted to know if Jasmine had heard any news. It was new, this sensation he had, as though a hole tried to burn its way through the pit of his stomach. Fear, he realized. He was afraid for her daughter. Worried that Jasmine had made him leave early because she didn't want to see him again. That concerned him most of all. He knew she'd made him leave so the girls wouldn't see him. The last thing Jasmine needed were questions that might lead to more difficult questions and inevitable curiosity on their part, but the fact that she hadn't called him? Well, that made the hole smoke a little more.

As it turned out his job helped him to put aside his fears. With Jasmine gone he ended up doing some of her tasks plus his own. Work kept him busy for the rest of the day. He kept checking for text messages, but there were none and it wasn't until he was about to head home that he finally gave in and sent her a text message of his own.

Dinner? he asked.

He was almost to the outskirts of Dallas when he finally heard his cell phone chime, but he had to wait until he reached a stoplight before glancing down.

Staying in tonight.

That was all she said. No "how was your day?" No "miss you." No "thanks for a good time last night."

Did you hear from the doctor? he typed next.

He waited for an answer, his heart suddenly racing off like a runaway bull. It was a long wait. Then he heard his phone sound her response.

Nothing yet.

His disappointment had to have been nearly as acute as her own. Damn. He almost dialed her number. Almost. Except…this morning had thrown him. The whole fear for another person thing. The way she'd sent him on his way. It was a lucky escape, wasn't it?

Wasn't it?

Too bad, he typed instead.

His fingers hovered over the tiny keypad. Should he ask to come over? He released a sigh of frustration. Why did he feel so out of sorts? He'd had sex with a woman. It appeared all she wanted was a one-night stand. Perfect. He was famous for one-night stands. That's what he liked. Nothing too serious. No commitment. No talk of the future. And yet…and yet….

He scrubbed a hand over his chin.

He wanted to see her again. Wanted to see Brooke,

too. Wanted to reassure himself that they were all right, and it scared the shit out of him.

He tossed the phone on the passenger seat. Next move was hers. If she wanted to see him, she'd ask to see him. She was that type of woman—straightforward and to the point. She'd keep him updated on Brooke, too. He had no doubt about that. He'd get over this weird reaction.

She didn't text him back. Nor did she call. He heard through the grapevine the next day that she'd taken another day off, with Lizzie's blessing of course. He broke down, though, and tried calling her once, and when she didn't answer, left an upbeat "hope everything's okay" message that sounded pathetic even to his own ears. She sent him an email in return, purely professional, explaining that they didn't have a diagnosis yet, but that she expected to return to the office the next day. He'd been incensed at how impersonal she'd sounded until he reminded himself that he should be glad. Lucky escape. Clearly, she didn't expect commitment. That was a good thing.

He might not have heard anything else but for Lizzie who popped her head into his office later that day and said, "I probably shouldn't be telling you this, but J.C. just called. Brooke is in the hospital."

He shot up so fast he damn near tipped his chair back. He caught the back of it just in time, but not without it bouncing on the plastic mat first.

"What's wrong with her?"

"I don't know."

"I need to know." It shocked him and completely frazzled him to realize how badly he wanted to go to them.

Lizzie stepped back and crossed her arms. "You're going to the hospital, aren't you?"

He stared at his sister for a long time, tried to understand what this strange, unnatural sensation might be. "She might need me," he heard himself say.

"If she wanted you there, she would have called you."

Her words brought him up short. They even stung a little. She was right. He *hated* when his sister was right. "I'll bring her flowers." He brushed past his sister before she could stop him.

"Jet."

He kept walking.

"Be careful."

The words brought him up short. He paused in the middle of a long hallway, photographs of their projects hanging on the wall, and he realized this was the tipping point. This was the moment where he either sank or swam. The trouble was, he had no idea if he could cross that ocean, if he even had a right to cross that ocean. He knew his foibles, knew his flaws, knew he wasn't the best at being there for people. Jasmine and her girls was serious stuff. If he went to her he was doing more than just visiting her in the hospital—he was making a commitment.

"Oh, dear," he heard Lizzie say.

Jet's chin shot up.

"It's finally happened."

"What?"

Lizzie smiled, and if he wasn't mistaken, there was moisture in her eyes. "And with an employee, too. Damn it, Jet."

"What?" he said again.

"Never mind. Go. I can tell you want to. Just go, and for the love of God, don't break her heart."

It was the first bit of advice he could remember accepting from Lizzie in years.

"I won't."

And he wouldn't. He headed toward the hospital, although not without stopping at a local florist first where he purchased a giant pink stuffed horse, one that lay on the ground as if sleeping, its golden princess bridle and saddle encouraging child riders. He reassured himself with the thought that no matter what, Brooke would appreciate his gift.

Brooke.

Worry gnawed at his gut. Whatever he might be feeling inside about the sick little girl would be nothing compared to Jasmine. Poor thing. She'd already been through so much what with the loss of her fiancé and before that her dad and before that, her mother. He couldn't imagine what must be going through her mind.

It wasn't hard to find the pediatric ward. Even if he hadn't known what floor it was on he would have found it by the life-size replica of Shrek that stood in the corner of the reception area, not to mention the colorful designs on the wall. Disney characters cavorted with cartoon characters, all of them meant to bring a smile to a child's face during a time when all they felt was fear. It damn near broke his heart.

"Can I help you?" asked a perky-looking blonde that couldn't be much older than him, the smock she wore nearly the same color as her eyes.

"I'm looking for Brooke Marks's room—"

"Jet?"

His whole body jolted to the core just from the sound of her voice. He turned, and any doubt he'd made the right choice in coming to the hospital was erased the moment he caught sight of her crumbling face.

"Jazzie," he heard himself say softly, not even sure where the endearment came from, but it didn't matter because in the next instant, he had her in his arms, giant horse and all, and he held her tight…and everything went back to right.

SHE'D BEEN KIDDING HERSELF. As she led Jet to a private waiting room, Jasmine admitted to herself that keeping her distance hadn't done one iota of good in lessening her feelings for the man. Not at all.

"I had a hard time waking her up this morning," she said, taking a seat near a window that overlooked the Dallas skyline. She watched as he set the horse—an enormous pink toy with golden tack—on the chair next to him. "I thought she was just tired at first, but then she wouldn't open her eyes…."

She bit back the rest of the words, so afraid she would break down and cry, something she refused to do. Brooke would be okay. Whatever was wrong with her, they would know quickly now. The results of her blood work and test had all been rushed thanks to their trip to the hospital. The waiting game would soon be over.

"Do they have any idea what it is?"

She shook her head. "They took a urine sample when she first came in, and more blood, but I haven't heard back."

"That must have been fun."

She smiled ruefully. "She worked herself up into such a state that when it was all over, she went right back to sleep." Which worried her all over again, but she wouldn't dwell on that. "I've been pacing the hallways ever since."

"What about Gwen?"

"Back at home with Mrs. Dalton, the lady who watches them during the day."

The panic threatened to clog her throat again, but she battled it down. She'd gotten good at that in recent days.

"I should get back to her."

"Here." He thrust the horse at her. "It's for Brooke."

She smiled. "I figured."

"I just thought I'd drop it by, you know, see how you were holding up."

"Jet—"

"Ms. Marks?"

Jasmine spun, the walls seeming to curve inward when she spotted Dr. Johnson, the pediatrician on call that day, standing in the doorway. "Good news. We have a diagnosis, although I had a pretty good idea what might be wrong when we tested her urine this morning. Dr. Lee did, too. I talked to him this morning and he suspected the same thing."

What? Jasmine wanted to scream. *What?*

"Her blood work confirms it. Diabetes."

Jasmine almost sagged to the ground. Diabetes. Not cancer. Not some horrible disease that would take yet another thing she loved.

"Type 1, unfortunately, which means your little girl's got a long period of adjustment ahead of her."

"But it's manageable, right?"

The doctor smiled. "It should be, yes. There are a lot of alternatives to treatment these days. The guesswork is figuring out what kind and how much insulin to give her. Metabolisms respond differently to different things, but we'll sort it all out. She should be feeling better within a week or two."

Oh, thank God.

"It's going to be a learning curve, though, and a dramatic change to your lifestyle. When we discharge her in a day or two she'll go home with a lot of medicine. I would encourage you to do your own research, as well."

"So she'll start treatment today?"

"Absolutely. She was severely dehydrated when she came to us this morning. That was the source of the lethargy. This afternoon we'll add insulin to her drip, see how she responds, but I suspect she'll do well. Compared to how she's been feeling lately, she'll probably be a handful by the end of this week."

She almost closed her eyes.

"Thank you."

She felt Jet's hands on her shoulders, their familiar touch causing her eyes to close at last. "Thank you," she said again, although she wasn't certain if it was Jet or the doctor she spoke to the second time. All she knew was that when Jet turned her around, she sank into his arms. And when he wrapped his long limbs around her, she was comforted by his embrace. Listening to the sound of his heartbeat beneath her ear was one of the most reassuring sounds she'd heard in a long while. Or maybe the peace she felt was knowing that Brooke would be okay. They might have some ups and downs ahead of them, but it would be okay. She wasn't going to lose her little girl.

When she started crying she had no idea, but she was horrified to realize the snuffling sounds came from her. She had to stop doing this, she thought. Since she'd met Jet Baron she'd cried more than she had in her whole life.

Jet. Her lover.

She'd tried to forget that this week. She'd been trying to do the responsible thing. The man was her boss. Her kid might be seriously ill. The last thing she needed was to dive into a relationship, boss or no boss. Yet here he was and she was grateful, so totally thankful.

"I'll leave you two to it," she heard the doctor say.

"Thanks," Jet answered for her.

She leaned back and met his gaze. "Jet, I'm so sorry I didn't call you this week."

"Shh. It's okay. I understand."

"No, it's not okay. I didn't think it was fair to drag you into all this with me. I've been down this road before. My dad. He died slowly. The stroke shut his body down little by little and it was horrible, just horrible to watch." She shook her head at the memory that flashed through her mind like pixels in a bad picture. Her dad, once so robust. Her dad a few weeks later—dead. "I just didn't..." She swallowed. "I didn't want to break your heart, too."

She saw him look away, saw his Adam's apple bob as he swallowed, and she realized that her words had affected him deeply. His eyes grew red, almost as if he fought back his own tears. "I do understand what it's like to lose someone, Jasmine. I guess I just sort of forgot."

She wondered who he'd lost, but she supposed it didn't really matter.

"I'm so sorry," she said.

"I'm sorry, too." He met her gaze again, then shook his head. "I should have made more of an effort. I was just scared—scared for you," he said quickly. "You've been through so much for someone so young."

Some days it felt as if she had a black cloud hanging over her head, but she had learned not to dwell on her misfortunes. Just deal with them and move on. That was her mantra, but it didn't mean those losses and setbacks didn't add up and, yes, make her just a little bit jaded. She would have to work on that one.

"Let's go see Brooke," she said.

She saw him take a deep breath, as if he fortified

himself for whatever might come in the future. She knew how he felt.

"Yes," he said. "Let's do that."

Chapter Fifteen

Brooke loved the stuffed horse. Jet would never forget the way the child's whole face changed when Jasmine gently woke her up and she spotted the giant toy. He'd thought seeing her so sick might be hard, but watching her face light up warmed his heart in a way he would have never thought possible.

"You do realize I'm going to have to get Gwen one of these, too."

Jet smiled. "I'll do that."

"No," Brooke said.

They both looked at the bed. Though she was sick, though there were dark circles beneath her eyes and she seemed as pale as Casper the Friendly Ghost, she was not too sick to feel competitive.

"Gwen doesn't need one," she announced.

He glanced up at Jasmine for guidance.

"It's a competition thing. They always have to one-up the other."

"Not true," Brooke pouted.

Jet laughed. He doubted the little girl even knew what *one-up* meant, but she understood the context of her mother's words based on the way she hugged the horse close to her and frowned up at her mother. Well, as close as she could get what with a tube sticking out of her arm and a monitor on her finger. The room was huge with bright blue walls and a rainbow painted on the ceiling, but nothing could disguise it was a hospital ward. Brooke seemed so tiny in the plastic-and-metal bed common to hospitals, her upper body partly tilted. Jasmine must have braided her hair. With the strands pulled back her face seemed paler and thinner than he remembered, and Jet admitted he would have promised her anything at that moment.

And then Brooke said, "Gwen can't have anything." She said it with such vehemence Jet almost laughed. "She isn't sick."

"I don't think you're going to be sick for too long," Jet admitted.

Across the bed, Jasmine shook her head in disgust. "I think you're right."

"Don't get Gwen a horse," Brooke ordered.

"Okay, okay. I promise, I won't." He crossed his heart. "But I may need to promise her something in return. Maybe that horse ride I promised you guys."

That seemed to appease the child. At least she wasn't completely heartless.

"In fact, both of you can come to my ranch."

The child's gaze fell on her mom, as if silently asking if that was okay. Jasmine nodded.

"Okay," Brooke said. "We can go."

"Well, I'm glad my plan meets with your approval."

And he was. He felt ten pounds lighter now that he'd seen the little girl, and that shocked him. He'd never really given kids much thought. There was a part of him that had wondered if he'd even have any. Yet here he was, worried sick about Jasmine's little girl. It sobered him for a moment.

He met Jasmine's gaze. "I should get back to the office."

Jasmine's own eyes grew worried. "Is everything okay there?"

"It's fine. We'll be ready to start drilling for oil next week. You'll be back just in time to witness all the fun."

She nodded. "Tell your sister that I'm so sorry."

"For what?"

Jasmine shrugged, then glanced down at her little girl. "I feel bad. I haven't even been an employee very long and here I am taking time off work."

"It's okay. She understands."

"Does she?"

"She does, trust me."

That seemed to reassure her. "Tell her I'll be in just as soon as things are settled with Brooke."

He followed her gaze. Brooke had closed her eyes again, the poor thing appearing exhausted after her outburst, her lashes fanned out against the dark circles beneath her eyes. Still, she hugged her horse as if she feared it might gallop away. The sight made Jet's throat tighten.

"I'll do that."

He wanted to go around the end of the bed and give Jasmine a kiss goodbye, but he didn't think that was a good idea. In the end it was the sight of her leaning forward and stroking a lock of hair off Brooke's face that stopped him. She needed to focus on her child.

"I'll call you later," he said instead.

She spared him hardly a glance. "Thanks for dropping by."

He left before he could give into the urge to offer to stick around for a bit. When he returned to the office there was a message from Lizzie asking how Brooke was. While it didn't surprise him, it did give him hope that maybe she was coming around, and that she really did understand. Not that he ever doubted it.

The rest of the day flew by for him. When he sent Jasmine a text he received a response right back that Brooke was doing great, but wanting to go home. She'd be there one more night. He would have dropped by that evening but he'd promised Lizzie he'd attend a state-mandated seminar on safety with his brother Jacob. Unfortunately, it was all the way down in Houston, something he'd completely forgotten about until Lizzie reminded him of it. He tried to wiggle out of it, but there was no way to do that. As Lizzie explained, the class was only offered twice a year, which meant he needed to go now. Just mentioning bowing out had made Lizzie breathe fire.

So he left town with Jacob although Jasmine promised to keep him updated, something that made him feel marginally better. He would have preferred to have been there when Brooke was discharged. It wasn't in the cards. And then Lizzie called and asked them to meet with one of their engineers while they were in Houston. The week never seemed to end. Doctors' appointments, problems at the job site and his own schedule.

"When are you coming home?" Jasmine asked him late Thursday night.

"Tomorrow."

"Good." He heard the smile in her voice. "I can throw some steaks on the barbecue for dinner."

He winced. "Actually, I have a rodeo tomorrow night. Evening performance. You should bring the girls."

Silence. "I'm not sure Brooke will be up to that."

Was she mad? Women usually loved watching him compete.

She wasn't most women.

"Why don't you bring the twins out to my place on Sunday?"

Silence again, but not as long this time. "Okay."

He couldn't shake the feeling that he'd somehow disappointed her, so he tried to soothe her. "I miss you."

He heard her sigh. "I miss you, too."

For the first time he almost regretted his rodeo life. It didn't even matter that he won both rounds and came home with a buckle. Honestly, he was more excited about Jasmine coming over. He felt like a kid waiting for his favorite sports figure to make an appearance as he stood looking out the picture window of his single-story ranch house two days later, waiting for them to arrive. He lived down the road from Roughneck—the Baron family ranch—far enough away that he didn't see them all the time, yet close enough that it made it easy to use Roughneck's equestrian facility when he needed to practice for rodeos. His family was wonderful. They were also annoying, nosy and overbearing at times.

A truck turned into his driveway.

His heart did that odd little skip-a-beat thing. His place was set back off the road, white vinyl fencing framing both sides of the driveway, irrigation providing for green pastures. It was Baron land and had been for generations. But he'd actually paid his dad for it and so it was his and he was happy—okay, excited—about showing it off to Jasmine.

He didn't want to examine the reasons why too closely.

"You made it," he called out when Jasmine's door opened a few moments later.

She slipped out, her blond hair loose and down her back, her blue eyes so dang gorgeous Jet flashed back to their first meeting and how struck he'd been by them even back then.

"Are you kidding? We couldn't get here fast enough for Brooke."

She opened the smaller door of her crew cab, and Jet spotted Brooke in the backseat. He knew it was her because she still clutched the massive stuffed horse he'd bought her, straw cowboy hat in place, blond hair just like her mother's pulled into a ponytail. And if his heart had skipped a beat earlier, it positively melted when he saw the little girl's wide smile. Who would have thunk? Jet Baron, happy to see kids.

"Hi, Jet," she said, legs kicking in excitement.

"Brooke," he said, stopping behind Jasmine. "How you feeling?"

"She's fine," Gwen answered for her, leaning forward so they could make eye contact. "Don't know what all the fuss was about. It's not like she was going to die or anything."

"Gwen!" Jasmine cried. "That's a horrible thing to say."

"It's true," the child said, a frown on her face as she leaned back.

"You're just jealous because *I* have Guinevere," Brooke said, tugging on the horse, which took up the entire space between her and her sister, toward her.

"Well, Mommy said I could be the first to ride a horse today, so there." Gwen stuck her tongue out at her sister, then began to fumble with the button of her car seat.

Jasmine turned toward him with an expression of long-suffering patience. "It's been like this since Brooke got home yesterday."

Brooke had gotten her own belts undone, but not all the way, and her impatience was expressed with a growl of frustration just before she said, "These belts drive me *nuts*," and the words sounded so adultlike, yet her voice so little and childlike, it was all Jet could do to keep a straight face.

"Here," Jasmine said, moving forward. "Let me help you."

"No, no, no, I've got it."

Four going on forty. Compared to his little stepbrother, Alex, they sounded positively grown-up, and yet there was only a year's difference between the three of them. Maybe boys really do mature slower than girls.

"There," Brooke announced, the buckle releasing at last. "Come here, Guinevere. We're going to meet a *real* horse."

"No, no," Jasmine said, holding up her hands. "Leave the horse here."

Gwen stood up, so small her head didn't even reach the top of the truck's roof. "There, you see, Brookie, you can't even bring Guinevere out of the truck. I told you not to bring her."

"I have to leave her here?" Brooke looked past her mother and found Jet's gaze. "Do I have to?"

He would have promised her the sun, the moon and a few dozen galaxies if he could have gotten away with it. Alas, Jet knew better than to countermand Jasmine's order. "I'm afraid so, sweetie."

The little girl appeared heartbroken, and Jet couldn't get over how much better she looked. He hadn't noticed it before, but there really was a difference between her and Gwen. Brooke was skinnier, something attributed to the diabetes Jasmine had told him, and so her face wasn't as plump. The circles beneath her eyes, so prevalent in the hospital, had faded, too. And she seemed to have lost her shyness.

"She sure does love that horse," he said.

"Yes, she sure does."

"She's not afraid of me anymore, either."

"You might long for the old days in a few hours," she said wryly.

"I guess giving a child a giant stuffed toy goes a long way toward building trust."

"Yeah, well, I wish you'd picked something a little smaller. I swear the thing needs its own car seat."

"I still say I should get another one."

Jasmine helped Brooke from the car, the child immediately setting off. "You take it easy," she called out because Brooke had spotted his horse over by the side of his house and she was headed right toward it. "You only just got out of the hospital." She turned back to the truck to help Gwen down, but she met his gaze first. "You get another one and *you* can cart it around."

"Wait for me!" Gwen called, jumping down next. She shot past her mother and ran to catch up to her sister.

"The thing's hell at a grocery store," Jasmine added. "Everyone makes a big fuss over it. Gwen's so jealous she would have flushed the whole thing down the toilet if she could have made it work." Her gaze focused past him, spotting the brown-and-white horse at the fence. "Don't get too close," Jasmine warned.

They'd reached the horse's head. "They'll be fine," he said. "Tuck is about a hundred years old. My old high school rope horse. He's like an equine babysitter."

Jasmine watched as the girls held their hands out, the big paint dropping his head and seeming not to mind in the least that two girls started to rub his hair the wrong way.

"I just worry."

"Of course you do. You're their mother."

She glanced up at him sharply. "They're my whole world."

Was she trying to tell him something? "I know. But I'm serious about getting a second one for Gwen."

"No." She shook her head. "Brooke needs to feel special now. She's been through a lot. Gwen will get over it."

She still stared up at him intently, and Jet wondered what it was he saw in her eyes. He committed the image of her to memory so he could examine it later. "How is Brooke feeling today?"

"Good. Better. She had an absolute fit today when I had to give her a shot, but she'll get used to it."

It was Jasmine who looked tired. She was still beautiful in her white, button-down top and her dark blue jeans, but Jet could tell the week had left her exhausted.

"How about you?"

She tipped her head. "Me?"

"Are you okay?"

She opened her mouth. He thought for sure she'd deny it, but then her eyes softened. "I'm okay."

He moved forward, fully intending to pull her into his arms, but she moved out of the way. His arms fell back to his side.

"Not now." She shook her head. "Not yet. Brooke's had enough shocks for one week."

He told himself he understood, but deep down inside he knew he didn't. He wasn't sure what it was he felt for Jasmine, but this wasn't some kind of casual fling, he knew that now. That day when he'd had to decide whether he'd go to her in the hospital had been something of an eye-opener for him. He was about to tell her about it except the sound of a car slowing down on the main road caught his attention. He glanced up and his stomach dropped.

"Damn."

Jasmine followed his gaze. A white truck pulled into the gravel driveway, the noonday sun catching on the paint and turning it gold, the tires kicking up a plume of dust. If he had any doubts about who it was they faded when they spotted the man in the cowboy hat.

"Who's that?"

"My brother Jacob."

Chapter Sixteen

"Well, well, well, what have we here?"

Jasmine cheeks flamed with color when she spotted the tall cowboy who slid from the white Baron Energies truck. Jacob Baron, Jet's brother and coworker. Her coworker, too.

"Dropping off some papers from work?" Jacob's eyes twinkled like birthday candles, all the proof she needed that he was just teasing. "Or did Jet tell you he has a well he'd like drilled in the back pasture?"

"It's nothing like that," Jet said, glancing in her direction. Something in his eyes warned her not to give too much away. She'd suspected Jacob hadn't known about her and Jet, but the look in Jet's eyes confirmed it. He hadn't said a word to his family. She wondered how much Lizzie knew—and why that made her stomach tumble end over end to think that Lizzie might know everything.

"I told Jasmine to bring her twins over this weekend. One of them just got out of the hospital, and I thought it would cheer her up."

Jacob tipped back his cowboy hat. "Really."

He didn't ask it like a question. No. He pronounced the one word like he knew damn well and good there was more to it than that.

"We just found out my daughter Brooke has type 1 diabetes," Jasmine added.

The teasing look in Jacob's eyes faded. "Is that the insulin kind?"

"Unfortunately for my daughter, yes."

He glanced between the two of them. "Too bad."

"It is," Jet said. "But I was about to saddle up Tuck there." He pointed with his chin to the paint horse in the pasture. "The old boy could use the attention."

Another searching gaze. "I'm surprised you didn't bring them over to the Roughneck. Brock and Julieta wouldn't have minded."

"I didn't want to bother them."

Nope. Jacob hadn't been told about them. Jasmine couldn't quite identify the bubbles of emotion that rose to the surface of her consciousness, but they were there. She supposed she should have been grateful to Jet for not telling the whole world they were an item.

Or *were* they an item?

Her gaze hooked on Jet and for the first time she acknowledged she didn't know what they were. Clearly Jacob didn't know, either, but he was curious.

"I came by for that rope you were telling me about at the high school rodeo. The softer Cactus Ropes one that you used to beat me in the team roping."

Jet laughed a little and smiled. "Yeah, sure, although I probably shouldn't be giving up my trade secrets. It's in the trailer."

Jet left her there without a backward glance, although Jasmine followed at a distance, more so she could be closer to the twins than anything else. She drew up short when she caught sight of the massive horse rig parked alongside the house. The thing was huge, almost the same length as his house. As was the truck that appar-

ently pulled the RV-like horse trailer. Both vehicles together looked more like a big rig. She had a feeling his
house was also huge. It was only one story, but the roof
was pitched at a steep angle, three dormers across the
front, a balcony around the exterior, including the side
of the house where they were standing. Lush landscap-
ing spoke of a professional's touch, red roses along the
front, an emerald-green swath of lawn in the center of
a turnaround driveway. The quintessential Texas ranch
right down to its name—JB Cattle Company—hung between twin telephone poles across the front.

"Mommy, look."

She turned back in time to watch Brooke feed Jet's
horse a blade of grass. Out in a field behind the horses
she could see multiple Black Angus eating in an irri-
gated pasture. No doubt Jet's cattle. But no big horse facility. She wondered about that. Jet competed regularly
on the rodeo circuit. All around, meaning roping and
riding, although she'd heard roping was his specialty.

"Watch your fingers," she said when Brooke didn't
let go of a piece of grass quickly enough. Fortunately,
the horse seemed to understand the difference between
fingers and forage.

She glanced up at Jet again. He'd entered through
a door on the side of the trailer and returned moments
later. He handed his brother a pink rope that would have
embarrassed a ballerina it was so bright. Jacob took it,
and his expression of glee was almost comical.

"Hot, damn. This baby ought to do the trick."

He unfurled the thing and flung it forward like a yo-
yo, whipping it back in such a way that it made a buzz-
ing sound reminiscent of a zip-tie being cinched down.
Clearly, the brother was a professional, too. She'd heard
that. She'd also heard that if Jet had applied himself to

roping like Jacob had applied himself to rodeo, Jet could have gone all the way to the World Championship.

"Go ahead and keep it," Jet said. "I have more where that came from."

"I bet you do." Beneath his cowboy hat Jacob had the look of a man who'd been given the keys to the kingdom. "Thanks, bro." He tugged the rope back in his direction, coiling it in a matter of seconds.

"What's that for, Mommy?"

She'd been so engrossed in watching the two men that she hadn't even noticed Gwen had lost interest in the horse. Not so, Brooke. Her youngest child couldn't take her eyes off the animal.

"He's a roper, honey."

"What's a roper?"

Jacob must have heard them because he turned toward Gwen and said in a falsely menacing tone, "We catch baby cows."

"Why?" Her daughter looked so horrified and so perplexed that it made Jasmine smile.

"Because they weren't listening to their mother."

Her daughter's mouth dropped open before she clapped it shut. The two cowboys moved nearer. Jasmine glanced at her other daughter. Brooke still fed the horse. Jacob, however, had unraveled his rope again, waving it in Gwen's direction.

"So you better be good, little lady, or I'll rope you, too."

He took a quick step in Gwen's direction. Her daughter yelped and ducked behind her leg. Jasmine laughed, placing a hand on her daughter's head.

"He's just teasing, honey." Gwen glanced up at her, her face full of concern. "I promise. He's not going to rope you."

"Yes, I will."

Jacob ran at her daughter, but Gwen had caught on. She squealed in delight, running for the front of the driveway. Jacob gave chase as Jet walked up beside her.

"He's good with kids," she observed.

"Yeah," Jet said, sounding as perplexed as her daughter. "He is."

She suspected that Jet would be good with kids one day, too. He'd already come a long way from the man who'd stared at her with such obvious consternation when Brooke had had her fit. That look would have worried her except that later on that same day she'd watched Jet with the older high school kids. She'd watched what seemed like half his family, all of them exhibiting a kindness that had taken her by surprise. The family was rich. She had no idea why she'd thought that meant they'd be self-absorbed because clearly they weren't. Even his sister Carly had helped out, as Jasmine had learned that even girls rode bulls these days.

"You should bring the girls out to the ranch to ride," Jacob said, coming back a moment later, Gwen giggling as she followed behind. "They'd have more fun riding the ranch horses than that old nag." He motioned toward Jet's old horse. "That thing's about dead."

"That's the point," Jet said. "They'll be safe."

"Nah. They'll be bored. Bring them by. I'm sure Brock wouldn't mind."

The stricken look on Jet's face told Jasmine all she needed to know. His father didn't know about them, either. That was good, she told herself. She didn't want the patriarch of the family to know that his son had gotten involved with one of his employees. Or maybe he did know. Maybe Lizzie had told him of her suspicions. That would be horrible. It had taken her forever to find a job. In a male-dominated world, CEOs were always worried about interoffice affairs. And, look, she'd gone and done exactly as all those male CEOs had feared. She should be ashamed of herself.

And yet...

"Seriously," Jacob said. "Family dinner's on Sunday. You should come."

"I don't think Brooke will be feeling up to that," Jet answered for her.

He was right, although she'd improved by leaps and bounds now that Mommy wasn't poisoning her with pieces of peach pie and muffins and sweet cereal in the morning. Jasmine didn't want to examine that thought too closely, not when her guilt had just about eaten her alive during Brooke's stay in the hospital.

"Thanks for the invite." She smiled at Jacob. "But Jet's right. I don't think Brooke will be up to it."

She glanced up at Jet just in time to see his expression of...relief? When he glanced down at her she knew that's exactly what it'd been.

Don't read too much into it. Maybe he's just trying to preserve your reputation at Baron Energies.

That must be it. He didn't want her reputation at work to suffer. She appreciated that. She didn't want people privy to her personal life. Far from it. Plus, when it came right down to it she was keeping him a secret, too—from her kids.

But that wasn't the same thing, she told herself. Her girls were young. They'd never seen Mommy with a man before. It would be an adjustment, one she'd been determined to take slow. This was different. This was a man not wanting her to meet his family and she couldn't help but wonder why.

"WHAT'S THE MATTER?" They'd just come in from riding old Tucker. Jet had expected Jasmine to be more relaxed. The girls sure were happy. Instead, she seemed pensive and almost sad. "You haven't seemed yourself since Jacob left."

They sat on bar stools that had been tucked beneath the island in the middle of his kitchen. Behind them the girls were drinking water and munching on pretzels. They were completely engrossed in rehashing every moment of their ride on Tuck.

"Jasmine?"

She frowned and shook her head.

He shifted on his cowhide seat, trying and failing to read what was in her eyes.

"Are you hungry, too? Do you want me to throw some steaks on the barbecue? I have half a cow in my freezer. Seriously. One of the perks of living on a ranch. A never ending supply of meat."

She wrinkled her nose as if the thought of killing a cow were foreign to her. "Brooke's on a special diet. It wouldn't be fair not to eat the same thing as her."

For some reason her words concerned him even more. "I'll come over to your place, then. That is, if you don't mind me inviting myself over."

She glanced around his kitchen—her gaze catching on the oak cabinets and the granite countertops—before landing on the girls again. He saw her take a deep breath before she looked him square in the eye and asked, "What are we doing?"

He must have looked as confused as he felt because she said, "You and I, Jet. What are we doing? Are we in some kind of relationship because if we are, I'm not so certain that's a good idea."

At last he understood, and he had to admit, he appreciated the way she confronted an issue, the way she simply stated what was on her mind. It amazed him, really. He'd never met a woman like her.

"I think we take this one day at a time," he said by way of an answer.

He saw her glance at her girls, saw her take another deep breath. "I worry about my girls."

"I know."

"Do you, Jet? Because I don't want them getting hurt."

"They won't, but I think we need to be open about what's going on."

"What do you mean?"

He shook his head. "I'm tired of acting like you're just a friend from work. Tired of having to make excuses to my family." He brought his head close to hers. "I think we tell them that we're dating, but that it's more of a casual thing...for now."

"And the girls? What do we tell them?"

He reached for her hands. "The same thing. We're friends."

"I don't want to confuse them. If you go around kissing me and touching me, they might not understand."

"I know. And I promise." He let her go and lifted his hands. "I'll keep these to myself."

She still didn't look convinced, and for some reason it threw him. He was used to women wanting to spend time with him, wanting to touch him. Sure, he rarely went on more than two or three dates with someone, but when he did, it wasn't a platonic thing.

"We would need to keep our private life private," he heard her say. "No hanky-panky in front of the girls."

He would take that. Hell, he would take her any way he could get her at this point.

"Agreed."

"Then we should probably eat back at my place," she said.

Was she propositioning him? He looked into her eyes, saw the gleam in them. She was.

But later, after they'd eaten at her place and the twins had had their baths and then been tucked into bed, he wondered about the uncertainty in her eyes. He tried to reassure himself by kissing her, but he had to wait until after the girls were asleep. It was hell, and when he finally did get to be alone with her, he didn't hold back. She was hesitant at first, but then something changed. She seemed to let herself go. Jet did the same.

They made love with an intensity that he knew he would never forget. And afterward, when she fell asleep in his arms, he held her, and as he did, the peace he felt was like none he'd ever experienced before.

When he awoke early in the morning, he left without being told. It was how the game would be played until....

Until *what?*

He honestly didn't know. He'd never been more confused and excited and terrified in his life. He didn't know where they were going. He was along for the ride.

Let's just hope you last longer than eight seconds.

He would, he reassured himself. He wasn't going to blow this. For once in his life he would take something utterly seriously. He had to, not just for Jasmine's sake, but for Brooke and Gwen's sake, too.

Chapter Seventeen

She went back to work that Monday. Thank God for Mrs. Dalton, who didn't bat an eye at Brooke's new diet. And thank God for Jet, who'd made sure her return to the office resulted in little stress. He'd covered for her while she'd been gone, and Jasmine had to admit he wasn't half-bad as a project manager. Not half bad at all.

Her week would have gone well but for one thing. Halfway through it she received a visit from none other than Julieta Baron herself, a woman she'd only ever seen from a distance, although not at the office. She'd spotted her at the rodeo although they'd never formally been introduced.

"You must be J.C.," she said with a wide smile, her olive complexion perfectly set off by a maroon business suit that hugged her voluptuous curves. A pencil skirt revealed legs that seemed to go on for miles, and all Jasmine could do was admire the woman's cool appearance when inside Jasmine felt as frazzled as the end of a rope.

"Mrs. Baron," she said, standing up and holding out her hand. "So nice to meet you."

"Same here." Dark eyes framed by dark lashes sparkled with friendliness and warmth. Jasmine could see why she'd been put in charge of publicity for the firm. It might be on a part-time basis but she would bet the woman's sweet smile had charmed more than the owner of Baron Energies.

"It's those darn part-time hours. I told Brock when Alex got older I would take on more hours, but that hasn't happened. Not yet, anyway."

"I know what it's like." Jasmine could only dream about working part-time. "Kids can be tough to leave behind."

"And you have twins." The woman motioned for her to sit back down while she took her own seat. "I can't imagine what that must be like."

She'd swept her thick black locks into a ponytail. Jasmine had pulled her own hair up in a knot, but she could tell some of it had come loose. Brooke had clung to her this morning and caught some of the strands as she'd been on her way out the door.

"It can be challenging at times." The smile she shot the woman was one of rueful amusement. "But I wouldn't change it for the world."

"Me, either, but speaking of kids, Jacob tells me you had your girls out to Jet's house so they could ride."

Jasmine didn't know what to say. She and Jet had agreed to tell people they were friends, but she hadn't counted on them being outed by Jet's brother. "I did."

"I was thinking you should bring them over this weekend while we're branding the fall calves. Your girls would love it and my son will be there. It'd be nice to have someone there for him to play with."

She knew what this was. It wasn't an invitation to a playdate. It was a way to gauge what was going on between her and her stepson. A test even. Maybe even a way to scare Jasmine off.

"Um…"

Think, Jasmine, think.

"Sure. That would be great." This was the boss's wife, after all, and Jet's stepmother. She couldn't exactly say no.

"Great." Julieta stood. "We'll see you on Saturday, then. Ask Jet for directions."

So clearly the word was out that Jet had a friend. How close of a "friend"? That was the question. That's what was behind the invitation.

She made sure the woman was well and truly gone before she dialed Jet's cell. Now that they had broken ground, he was pretty much out at the job site nonstop. That actually worked in their favor.

"What's up, beautiful?" he answered after a single ring.

She took a deep breath. "Guess who just came by my office?"

"Well, I don't know." She could hear the smile in his voice. "The Easter Bunny?"

"Julieta."

Silence. She could hear the rhythmic pounding of the hydraulic drill in the background. Now that everything had been approved and was in place, there was very little for her to do—not unless something went wrong.

"What did she want?

"I think I'm being summoned. Did you tell them about us?"

"No."

"Lizzie?"

"She might have."

Jet had confessed a few days ago that his sister had guessed they were more than casual friends. She hadn't exactly been thrilled, but the few times she'd bumped into Jet's sister, Lizzie treated her with the same friendly professionalism she always had. She'd even asked her about Brooke, smiling when she heard her daughter was doing much better.

"Should I bow out?" she asked.

"No. Don't do that. They'll think we've got something to hide."

She licked suddenly dry lips. "We do have something to hide."

Over the sound of the job site she could hear something that sounded like a sigh. "Just relax. It'll all work out."

She hoped he was right. This whole week she'd been worried he might see what her life was like with the girls and run in the opposite direction. Instead, he'd been supportive, sweet and even helpful.

She could get used to him being there all the time.

That was a thought she refused to dwell upon.

Saturday rolled around far too quickly. For some reason she was unaccountably nervous. Jet had told her to be herself. Easy for him to say. He'd had twenty-four years of being himself around his family. One thing she couldn't deny—her girls were beside themselves with excitement. They wore matching overalls, although Jasmine had put her foot down at finding them cowboy hats. She had broken down and bought them boots. When they'd seen Jet drive up, his own cowboy hat in place, they'd squealed in delight. It was all Jasmine could do to strap them into the car seats they'd moved from her truck to Jet's. It was early, not even seven, but that would be good because it had dawned a cloudless day and despite it being September she suspected it would be warm today.

"Will we get to ride?" Brooke asked for about the thousandth time.

"Maybe later," Jet answered, starting up his truck,

and looking far too handsome for his own good with half a day of scruff on his chin and a white T-shirt over his hard body. "We have some work to do first. You two will need to help fill the medicine guns."

"We get to hold a gun?" Gwen asked. When Jasmine glanced toward the backseat she nearly laughed at her daughter's wide eyes.

"Not that kind of gun, honey," she said. "And you won't be touching it, you're just going to help Jet put medicine in it."

Jet had explained the process. Her official job would be filling the syringes with vaccine, which involved injecting a needle in a bottle and sucking in the contents. The kids got to throw out the empty bottles—that was all. Cows had babies two times a year, in the spring and fall. The ones born in the fall would need to be moved to a winter pasture at some point soon, thus the need to castrate and vaccinate them. She'd had no idea there was such a thing as a "winter pasture," but apparently his family moved all their cattle to a ranch in New Mexico to graze during the cold season.

"So we won't get to shoot it?" This time it was Brooke who spoke, and she sounded disappointed.

"Nope," Jet answered. "No shooting guns."

They drove what seemed like hours, but that was probably her nerves acting on her sense of time. "How big is your family's ranch?"

"Big enough."

It must be big if he didn't want to admit to the actual number of acres. Plus, they were nowhere near the entrance to the ranch she'd seen when she and the girls had visited him. By her estimation they were at least a good half hour away to the south.

In her years out in the field she'd seen a lot of dirt

roads, but the one they eventually turned onto could hardly be deemed a road. The entrance lay between two old fence posts—wooden—barbwire strung to the left and right. All that marked the place were twin strips of dirt that had been worn into knee-high grass.

"If I didn't know better I would swear you were crazy," she said.

"Just wait."

She might not have grown up on a ranch, but she knew standard protocol was that the passenger always opened the gate. This one was galvanized, which meant it was light enough. You always left the gate as you found it, too, in this case closed, because if you left a gate open you risked the wrath of the ranch's owner. When she climbed back inside it was in time to hear Gwen say, "Can I get out of my car seat?"

"I don't know," Jet said. "Ask your mom."

"Not until we get there."

He took his eyes off the ghostly strips of dirt only long enough to say, "They'll be okay. It's just over that hill there."

What hill? But then she saw. The land wasn't as flat as she'd thought. A gentle incline had begun, one that grew more and more obvious the farther they drove. The top was lined with trees and Jasmine could tell by the condition of the grass on either side of the path that theirs wasn't the first vehicle to pass this way today. She saw why an instant later when they crested the top of the rise.

"Wow."

They had definitely been climbing. Below them lay a bowl-shaped meadow, with a creek on one side and cattle chutes on the other and all around were trees, their huge canopies leaving ink blots on the ground. Trucks and trailers and even a few cars were parked near where at least a hundred head of cattle were corralled. She could hear their cries of confusion, their babies huddled close to the mothers' sides, their own cries sounding so lost and forlorn.

"Look at all the cows, Mommy." Brooke was straining to see between the front seats.

"You can go ahead and unbuckle."

Her girls couldn't push buttons fast enough, the two of them standing up the minute they were free and leaning on the front seats, mouths open wide, eyes scanning this direction and that, excitement causing them to shift from foot to foot like horses in a starting gate.

"Why are they roping them?"

"What is that man doing?"

"Why are they so loud?"

"Why is that baby cow running?"

It was hard to tell which one said what but by the time they pulled to a stop beside a silver pickup Jasmine was smiling. She hadn't seen Brooke's cheeks flushed with color in weeks. Months, really, which made her wonder how long she'd been sick. She was feeling good today, that was for sure. There'd been the usual outburst this morning when she'd been given her insulin, but they'd gotten through it. In time, she'd get used to her treatments—or so Jasmine had been told.

"Okay," Jet said, turning off the engine and facing the twins. "Rules of the rodeo."

Both girls had instantly quieted. Her smile turned into a small chuckle. If only they would listen like that all the time.

"No climbing in the cattle pen." Jet wagged a finger at them. "You're to stay outside all the time."

Twin heads nodded, their ponytails swinging.

"No sticking your hands, ears, nose, toes or assorted other limbs into the pen, either, and definitely not the squeeze."

They both nodded again, but then Gwen spoiled the appearance of compliance by asking, "What's a squeeze?"

Jet swung around, pointing to a mechanism at one end of the corral. There were cowboys and cowgirls grouped around it, everyone wearing a weird kind of half chap that Jasmine hadn't seen before.

"That's it right there. Stay away from that."

Double nods.

"Over there is where we store the medicine. You see that table right by the squeeze? That's where you'll be standing. You're not to wander off. You're not to play between the parked trucks or cars and you are most definitely not to pet any of the horses tied to the trailers. They might not be as friendly as old Tuck."

"Are you riding, Jet?" Brooke asked.

He smiled. "Yup. Jacob brought my horse down from the ranch for me. He also loaded up a few of our other horses, and if y'all are good, we can go on a trail ride when we're done."

If he'd told the girls they were going to Disneyland they couldn't have screamed any louder. Jasmine wanted to cry. Two weeks ago she'd been afraid for her child's life. Now she was jumping up and down and whooping in delight and it made Jasmine's throat clog with tears.

"Okay, here we go," Jet announced.

Chapter Eighteen

"I like her."

Jet rested his hand on the horn of his saddle and followed Jacob's gaze to where Jasmine stood by the side of the corral. She appeared to be deep in conversation with Julieta at she filled up syringes, the two women laughing at something one of them said in between handing empty medicine bottles to the kids. Brock sat in the front seat of an all-terrain vehicle, giving out orders from inside the covered cab, grumpy as a badger with a stepped-on tail. Jet didn't blame him. While the pins were out of his leg, he still had a hard time getting around, and the uneven terrain of the pasture made it nearly impossible.

"She's not like the women you usually date," Jacob added.

Jet almost laughed. That was for sure.

They were in the cattle pen, resting their horses beneath a large tree. Their job was to ensure calves returned to the heifer pasture via an entrance at the end of the corral. Occasionally one would head in the wrong direction, toward the other calves in a holding pen at the opposite end. They'd use their horses to help push them in the right direction.

"She has a brain," Jacob added.

"Hey. Watch it."

They were both hot and sweating beneath their cowboy hats and white T-shirts. It'd been a long morning, but they were almost finished. Lunch would be soon.

"Seriously, Jet. You should be careful with that one."

Jet pulled his gaze away from a baby heifer they'd just released. "I know."

Jacob, too, rested his hand on the horn. "Do you?" His horse shifted beneath him, but his stepbrother didn't appear to notice. "She's not like the buckle bunnies you usually hang out with. She has twins."

Jet sat up straighter. "Believe me, I'm well aware of that."

It must have been Jacob who had told Julieta about Jasmine. He'd assumed Lizzie, but the look in Jacob's eyes had him wondering.

"If I didn't know better, I would swear you were warning me away."

Jacob's eyes went wide, but not out of guilt. "No, no. Like I said, she seems great. Lizzie speaks very highly of her. Well, aside from her taste in men."

"Hey."

Jacob shot Jet a smile. "I just…" For the first time in a long while, Jacob seemed a little lost for words. "I just want you to be careful. If things get serious—"

"You don't need to say it. I'm aware that it's not just Jasmine's heart I'm messing with, but her kids', too."

Jacob's whole face registered surprise. "Wow. Maybe you do get it. Glad to hear it. But that's not all I wanted to talk about."

"Oh, great."

Jacob ignored him. "I have some experience with what it's like to be given an instant dad."

He meant Brock, of course.

"Hell, a whole instant family, which if things get serious, those little girls will have, too. One minute it'll be just them and their mommy and the next it'll be all of us." He motioned toward all the people near the chutes. "It might be a little overwhelming."

"You make it sound like we gave you and Daniel a tough time."

"No. You didn't. Not at all. We—Daniel and I, we got lucky. Brock's been a great stepfather. When our mom died…"

Jet nodded. "Yeah, that was tough for me, too. I can only imagine what it was like for you."

"It's not easy losing a mother."

"At least you had one."

It was Jacob's turn to study him closely. "You sound like Carly."

"What do you mean?"

With a lift of his shoulders, Jacob said, "I overheard her talking to Savannah at the store. That's how I heard about the search for Delia, which Carly tells me didn't make you too happy."

He'd duly reported that knowledge to Brock, but Jacob was right. He still didn't get it. Brock had seemed relieved by his attitude, but Jet couldn't shake the suspicion that his dad hoped the whole thing would just go away. To be honest, he did, too.

"I just don't get it," Jet admitted. "The woman left us high and dry. They should just leave well enough alone." His horse shifted beneath him. He patted the gelding's neck. Talking about his real mom always upset him. His horse must have sensed that.

Jacob didn't say anything. That caused Jet to glance in his direction.

"I guess I never thought about the fact that your mom

walked out on you. That must have been tough," he admitted.

"I was a baby when it happened," Jet said. "You can't miss what you don't know."

"Yeah, but don't you ever wonder what she's like?"

"Nope. I want nothing to do with the woman. She left us and that's that. Look at Jasmine." He spotted her figure again, her bright blond hair like a beacon beneath the sun. "She could have terminated her pregnancy when her fiancé died. Or given them up for adoption. She didn't do that, though. She didn't leave them for someone else to raise."

"I didn't realize he'd died."

"She found out she was pregnant right after his funeral."

"Wow."

"One more reason why I would never hurt her."

"I know. I was just saying that, as someone who's been on the outside looking in, this family can be a lot to take on." He tipped his chin toward the group again. "You're lucky. The twins are young—they'll adjust, but it might be hard on Jasmine. Have the two of you talked about marriage yet?"

"Damn, Jacob, we're just friends."

Liar. They'd become a lot more than friends. It had started to worry him because he didn't know, wasn't really certain, if that's what Jasmine wanted. They'd agreed to take it slow, but they'd never talked about what might happen if slow turned into something more than slow.

"Yeah." Jacob picked up his reins, aiming his horse for a calf that headed in their direction. The thing changed directions at the last minute, though, heading for the out gate. He relaxed again. "I can see you're 'just friends' and so be careful, if not for Jasmine's sake, then the girls' sake. I remember what it was like to watch my mom date men. Didn't bug me when I was younger, but as I got older..." He shrugged again. "You've got to think about more than yourself."

"How's your day been?"

Jasmine looked up from the bowl of salad she was serving to the line of cowboys and cowgirls and then back at Jet. She'd been told they always did a buffet. Today it was ham, two types of salad—potato and greens—and dinner rolls. Lots of food for lots of people because it wasn't just the Baron kids at the branding, she'd learned. A whole score of their friends had shown up—neighbors, coworkers, old high school buddies. It was all hands on deck when you had a lot of cattle to doctor and brand and today was definitely one of those days, she'd learned.

"I'm doing good," she said with a smile, salad tongs in hand.

"Where are the kids?" he asked.

She pointed with her chin to a nearby tree. "Eating lunch with Alex."

Brooke and Gwen had taken an instant shine to Jet's youngest half brother. The three little kids were clearly enjoying themselves as they shoveled ham and potato salad into their mouths and giggled about goodness knew what.

"What about you?" Jet asked. "When are you going to eat?"

"After we're done serving."

She scooped some salad onto his plate and waved him on, but Julieta said, "No, no. You two should eat together. You're his guest."

Did she imagine the extra emphasis on "guest"? She stared into Julieta's warm brown eyes. No. The woman was just seeing to the needs of her stepson's friend.

"That's okay." Jasmine smiled at the cowboy standing next to Jet, an older man with a friendly smile. Everyone had been friendly today. At first she'd felt like an outsider, but everyone was so nice it was hard to feel like a stranger. "I'll catch up with Jet later."

"He should eat with you," Julieta said sternly. She set her spoon down, told the people in line she'd be right back, and returned with an empty paper plate which she shoved in Jasmine's direction. "Don't wait in line. Just fill it up here."

His sister Savannah was manning the ham station a few feet away and she leaned forward. "Here—" she motioned with her fork "—come get some of this."

"I think you better listen," Jet said. "They both look about ready to smack you with their forks."

"But—"

"Honey, I admire your work ethic," Julieta said, setting her tongs down and grabbing her by the shoulder and turning her, "but you're holding up the line."

Point taken, Jasmine thought. She clutched the plate Jet handed her.

"And don't you worry about those kids," Julieta called when they left the line, plates heaped with food. "I'll keep an eye on them."

A few minutes later they were settled beneath another tree, close enough to the kids to jump in if they were needed, yet far enough away that they'd been given some privacy.

"You been okay?" Jet asked.

"Yeah, sure."

Jet must have read something of what she'd been feeling earlier because he kept staring at her. "Jacob said we can be a bit overwhelming at times."

She rested her plate on her knees. "Only a bit?"

"I guess I never thought of it before."

Her girls giggled. Jasmine felt as if a million pounds of weight had been lifted from her at the sound. Brooke was doing so much better. Gwen was delighted by her surroundings, too. And who wouldn't be? How many times had she wished she could take them to a park so they could run and play? Unfortunately she didn't know the area well enough. This, however, was the best kind of park. Beautiful and stunning didn't begin to describe the trees and prairie grass around them. Even the afternoon heat didn't bother her. The smell of fresh grass and wildflowers was a balm to her soul.

"The water table must be pretty high in these parts."

He took a big bite of ham before saying, "Ever the geologist."

"Well, I do have a degree in geology, but it doesn't take a rocket scientist. The grass is so green it looks fake, and I don't see any dikes for irrigation, ergo, it must all be spring fed."

"It is."

"It's nice." She took a bite of her potato salad. "I could stay out here forever."

She was quiet as she waited for…

Waited for *what?*

Some type of commitment? Had she lost her mind? He'd trotted off to a rodeo this past weekend instead of coming to see her and the girls. If ever there was evidence that he didn't get what being in a relationship was all about, that was it. Yet here she was, wondering what he would say, if maybe he would give her a clue that they really were more than friends and that she maybe could stay on a ranch forever.

"Jet—"

"Did you see the way Alex tried to rope the girls earlier? Hilarious."

It was such an obvious change of subject that she drew back.

You love him.

No. Well, maybe. Good Lord, she didn't know what she felt, she just knew she'd been hurt when he'd chosen rodeo over her and her kids. She'd needed him. Had missed her lover, too.

"I saw the way the girls tried to rope him back. Did me proud. Who needs a man?"

His gaze shot to her own. "That sounded suspiciously like a warning."

Had it? Damn it, she felt as if she'd been tossed in a box, one that'd been flipped end over end so that she didn't know which way was up.

"I'm the daughter of a roughneck. I was raised to be strong and independent. My girls will be raised the same way. They won't be told they can't run a big corporation like your sister Lizzie."

He jerked as if she'd slapped him. "That's not fair. Lizzie's free to do whatever she wants."

"Hah." She picked up her plate, took another bite. "If you believe that you must believe in fairies, too. Everyone in the industry knows she's the best woman for the job when it comes to running Baron Energies, I mean, but your dad keeps holding out for you. So let me ask you a question, Jet. Would you give it all up? Rodeo. Jumping out of planes. Thrill seeking. Would you give it all up and stay at home—here in Dallas home—and hold down a nine-to-five job, support me and my girls?"

She'd thrown him. He hadn't expected such a serious question.

"Because that's where we are, I think. We need to decide. Friends? More than friends? What?"

"Jasmine…"

"No. Hear me out. I've worried since the day I met you that you might run in the other direction when things got too serious. I told myself not to worry because it would never get to that point, but I think it's headed that way. Don't you?"

He looked her square in the eye and said, "I do."

She stopped breathing.

"I hadn't thought about it before now, but I do, Jazzie. I think I'm falling in love with you."

Her lips began to tremble. "You are?"

He took her plate from her, set it down, cupped her face with his hands. "Jasmine Marks, I don't know what it is about you, but I know this past weekend I was miserable at that rodeo without you. I missed the girls, too. It felt off, almost wrong to be away from you three."

Something warm fell against her cheek. She didn't want to admit to herself what it was because she hated tears, but ever since she'd met him that was all she seemed to do. Cry.

"Jet—"

"I don't know where this is headed—maybe marriage, maybe not, but I—"

"You're getting married!"

Jasmine gasped. Gwen stood by them, mouth wide open. "Jet will be my daddy?"

"Gwen…"

"Hooray!"

And then her daughter threw herself into Jet's arms. She heard someone repeat what Gwen had said, one of the adults. Jet's sister Savannah came rushing over. Then Julieta. Brooke ran up to her, too, and Jasmine knew that whatever Jet had been about to say, whatever he'd been about to spell out for their future—she would never know. Everyone just assumed Jet had asked her to marry him. Jet seemed as flummoxed over the situation as she was. But then, as he accepted the congratulation of his family, his expression seemed to change. He gave her a look, one that seemed to say, "Well? What about it? You game?" And she tried to smile back, she really did. She even played along…for the girls' sake. She didn't want to disappoint them. Not yet.

But as she stood back and watched everyone react, she admitted she was terrified. She didn't want to disappoint her girls, but what if Jet did? What if she let it happen? What if she went along with their strange engagement and then Jet got cold feet? There was a good chance he would. She'd asked around, spoken to some of the girls at the office. They all said the same thing. Jet had never been serious about a woman in his life. He dated, but that was it. Now he was thinking marriage?

She was too much of a realist for that.

Men like Jet bounced through life as if it were a big party, but it wasn't. This was real. Her girls were counting on her and she owed it to them to be pragmatic.

Even if it meant letting go.

Chapter Nineteen

Okay, so as marriage proposals went, it wasn't exactly what Jet had had in mind. Actually, he hadn't had marriage in mind at all, but when he'd seen the look on little Gwen's face, when he'd spotted the joy in her eyes, he'd had the thought that maybe it was what he wanted. Maybe he was just scared. So when at last they were finally alone, the girls having taken forever to settle down they were so excited, he turned to Jasmine on her couch and said, "Well?"

"Well, what?"

"What do you think?" She looked away and Jet knew. "You don't think, do you?"

She glanced over her shoulder, toward the girls' room before turning to him and saying, "Let's go out on the balcony."

Yup. Just as he suspected.

"Yeah, sure," Jet said, but as he slowly stood up, his stomach flipped. He might have told himself he'd gone along so as not to disappoint the girls, but now that he'd seen a glimpse of the future in Jasmine's eyes, he knew the truth. He really had fallen in love with her. The girls, too, but she wasn't in love with him.

Jasmine led him toward the door, but she stayed out of reach. He didn't try to take her hand. Didn't touch her, just focused on putting one foot in front of the other. Ironic, really. The man everyone thought couldn't commit had fallen in love with a woman who wouldn't commit to him.

The door to the balcony opened with a *whoosh* of honeysuckle-scented air. A white balustrade seemed to glow in the moonlight. It was near midnight, that same moon painting Jasmine's hair with streaks of gold.

"Don't worry," he said. "I know what you've come out here to say."

He'd fallen, but she hadn't. He could tell by her face, and it killed him because he knew that for the second time in his life a woman was going to leave him.

"Jet…"

"Sit down," he said, patting the seat beside him on the wrought-iron park bench she'd placed outside. She sat next to him, but scooted away. She'd changed into jeans and a light blue sweatshirt that highlighted her eyes. She didn't speak, either. Not at first. She just sat there looking blonde and gorgeous and far too untouchable, and it was weird because his arms literally ached to hold her.

"I'm sorry," she said.

"Yeah," he said. "I'm sorry, too."

She looked away, out over the miniature park, the moon's touch turning her skin pearl-white. "It was just—"

Too fast.

She didn't need to say it, and he had to give her credit. Some women would be thrilled by an offer of marriage from him. They'd say yes because of his name, because of his family's wealth, because he had a good job and solid future. Not his Jazzie. None of that mattered to her.

"Earlier, things just sort of spiraled out of control. Gwen's never been quiet about anything, and then Savannah came running over and then your stepmother was there, I never had time…"

To set the record straight.

She didn't need to spell it out to him.

She stood and took a step away. "I care for you, Jet. I really do. A lot, but this is just too much. I'm still sorting out Brooke's health issues."

"Wait." He moved toward her. "You're not breaking up with me, are you?" Her gaze lowered, and he knew he had his answer. "I mean, we can go back to being friends, right?" Because he'd been hoping he could convince her, that with time he might get her to change her mind. They didn't have to tell anyone they weren't really engaged. They could pretend and keep on seeing each other. Right?

Wrong.

"It's not fair to my girls. You're the first man I've been involved with since they lost their father, not that they ever knew him, but that's my point. They've never had a man in their life. And then here I go, the first male I introduce them to and they're thinking fairy tale and Mommy's going to wear a pretty dress and that we'll all live happily ever after like we're in some kind of Disney movie."

"It *can* be like that."

"No, Jet. It can't. That's not reality."

For her.

Her past. The rotten hand of cards she'd been dealt, over and over and over again. She couldn't see past the burnt-out trees in the forest.

"So I'm going to quit…before this gets messy. Before I blow this so bad your sister won't recommend me to a local fast-food restaurant."

He wanted to reach out and pull her into his arms. "No."

But she was nodding. "I think it'd be for the best. I've worked for Baron long enough that your sister would give me a decent reference. I think she's seen enough of my work to know I'm good at what I do."

"Of course she knows that, but you can't quit."

He couldn't believe what she was saying, couldn't believe it'd come to this.

"I knew you'd say that," she said. "That's why I already sent your sister a text."

"You *what?*" His back had jerked upright. "When did you do that?"

"Earlier, when you went out to the truck to get Brooke's stuffed horse."

She turned away. He had to strain to hear her say, "She replied instantly. Told me she was sorry to see me go." She lifted her head. "Of course, she probably thinks I'm quitting because of our so-called engagement, but I'll set her straight in the morning. So it's all settled, but I wanted to thank you, Jet. You gave me a chance to prove myself at Baron Energies. I appreciate that."

She closed the distance between them, and when their gazes connected, he could tell she'd never been more serious about anything in her life. She really was calling it quits. Not just on him, but on everything.

She kissed him on his cheek. "I think you should leave."

"Don't do this, Jazzie."

But he came up empty when he reached for her. She retreated inside. He almost followed, thought about sleeping on the couch, but knew he was doomed. She was a stubborn woman, his Jazzie. Once she made up her mind, it was made up. He knew that.

But as he gripped the handle of her front door he paused and, damn it all, his heart seemed to stop working for a moment. His lungs, too. In the end, though, he walked out her door…and out of her life.

AN ENVELOPE SLAPPED her desk. "You can't quit."

Jasmine looked from the envelope—her official resignation letter, one that she'd typed up last night and left on Lizzie's desk this morning—as it skated across the glass surface of her desk and came to a stop a few inches away from her keyboard.

"I'm sorry, Ms. Baron, but I really feel I have no choice."

The woman didn't even wait to be invited to sit down. She just plopped down in the guest chair. Of course, she was seven months pregnant. "So it's Ms. Baron now, is it? This weekend it was Lizzie."

Great. Just what she needed. Her boss was mad at her, and she could tell by Lizzie Baron's tone that the coming conversation would not be pleasant.

"I just thought that since we're at the office I should be a little more formal with you."

"You thought wrong," said the woman who appeared the consummate businesswoman in yet another business suit, this one charcoal-gray, matching the thunderclouds in her eyes. She could see those eyes perfectly, even in the reflection of her desk. "I thought we were friends."

Jasmine gulped. "We were…are. And as your friend I should never have let things get out of hand with your brother. Yesterday, that was all a mistake. Gwen heard your brother mention marriage to me and she just assumed it meant we were getting married, but we're not. We lied to your family, and I'm sorry about that. It was highly unprofessional, and I'll understand if you don't want to give me a reference."

"You can't quit."

Whatever she'd been about to say, that wasn't what Jasmine had expected. "I beg your pardon?"

"Jet just bailed, too."

Her chair bounced she sat up so quickly. "He what?"

"He quit. Told me to keep the better person, which in this case meant you."

It was as if the floor came out from under her. Jasmine clutched the edge of her desk for support. "He can't do that. Your dad. He'll be livid."

Lizzie smirked. "Yes, he will be, but Jet can and he did, which means you're not going anywhere."

"I'll talk to him—"

"No, you won't. You'll leave him alone."

"But I can fix this—"

"You can't fix a broken heart and that's what you gave him." She ran a hand through her blond hair. "Jeez, Jasmine, you have no clue how hard my brother fell for you, do you?"

Actually, she did. She'd seen it in his eyes and it'd been that more than anything that had terrified her. He didn't know her well enough to love her. Didn't know her girls, either. He had no clue what it meant to be a parent. It would be irresponsible of her to accept that love.

"My brother," Lizzie said, "the quintessential philanderer. The man who couldn't take a brain tumor seriously, fell for you hard, and the bitch of it is that last week I would have told you both to cool your jets. This week I'm not so certain that's the right thing to do."

Cuss words. That couldn't be good coming from a woman like Lizzie Baron.

"I am *so* sorry."

"And so now I'm left with a choice. You or him. I know Jet won't let me boss him around, so you're it." She leaned toward her. "I'm making you the new project manager. It was my brother who suggested I promote you, but you really are the best person for the job, so there it is."

"You're promoting me?" The words were barely a whisper.

"As of today you're taking over Jet's job. I'll try to find a new engineer to replace you, hopefully before my dad finds out."

"This isn't right." Jasmine shook her head. "Jet's the one who should stay. I'm the one who let things get out of hand. He shouldn't pay the price for my mistake."

Lizzie sat there, and for a long time she didn't say anything. Jasmine didn't, either. She had a feeling the woman was taking a moment to size her up.

"Oh, believe me, I wanted to fire you for what you did to my brother. But I couldn't."

"Why not?" Jasmine heard herself ask as Lizzie turned to walk away.

She saw Lizzie freeze, saw her half turn back to her. For a moment she thought she'd ignore her, or that she'd pretend to misunderstand the question. But in the end she turned and faced her fully. "Because my brother asked me to promote you. Because he reminded me that you're a single mother of two. Because no matter what I might think of the situation you're in, you really are good at your job and my brother wants to make sure you're okay."

She couldn't breathe.

"Because he also reminded me what it was like to be

a woman in a man's world. But most of all because I love my brother and he asked me to do this for him, so I am."

The words made Jasmine want to cry.

Chapter Twenty

He entered every rodeo he could. Didn't matter if it was a small-time or a big-time professional rodeo. He just wanted to forget. If he could have, he would have entered a perf every night. Instead, he found himself practicing more and more.

"You know, you really don't have to do this."

Jet's grip tightened on the bar of rosin he held, Lizzie's voice bringing back the past and all the memories he sought to avoid. So he ignored her, hoping she'd go away, swiping the bar of rosin down the rope, then doing it again and again.

"If you're trying to kill yourself, there are easier ways."

"What the hell are you doing here?"

"You could step in front of a train, for instance, or maybe jump out of a moving car."

He sighed, then turned to face her. "Go away."

He was at a bull-riding practice and the fact that his sister had tracked him down made him all the more incensed. Despite being pregnant he could see the cowboys sneaking glances at her as if she were some kind of buckle bunny out to meet men. It wasn't a place he usually frequented, not when they had their own practice pen at the Roughneck, but for the past two weeks he'd shown up whenever he could. The bulls were ranker. More dangerous. More suited to his mood.

"I'm just sayin'. You don't have to climb on everything with four legs if you have a death wish."

He turned back to his rope, which he'd hung on the topmost rail that surrounded the arena. Nearby, cowboys and contractors gathered around the bucking chutes while bulls waited to be loaded into them through wooden alleys.

"I'm just trying to get in better shape. I lost focus for a few weeks, but not anymore."

"Bullshit. You're in great shape. You're just on the same path to self-destruction that you've been on ever since that woman dumped you."

"Her name is Jasmine, as you well know, and she had her reasons for doing what she did."

He went back to prepping his rope. It was important to get as much rosin as possible on the nylon strands. The pinesap made them sticky, and that stickiness kept the rope in place when wrapped around a hand, especially when it came in contact with a deerskin glove.

"Just like you had your reason for pushing her."

Ignore her.

"Or are you in denial about that, too?"

What was wrong with his sister? Didn't she get that he didn't want to talk about it?

"Because if you don't face reality now, Jet, you might find yourself in the same situation at some point in the future and I would hate to see that. I really would."

The sorrow in his sister's voice proved to be his undoing. "All right." He jerked around. "Whatever it is you came here to say, go ahead. Say it."

Even as a part of him fought off anger, even as a part of him wanted to shake his sister for pouring salt into his wounds, a part of him registered that he'd never seen Lizzie look so serious before.

"You drove her away."

He almost went back to working on his rope. "No kidding."

"Because you're so used to getting what you want, you didn't even stop to consider the consequences of pushing her like you did."

"I didn't push her. I took it slow."

"Not at the end, you didn't. You should have never let that sham marriage proposal go on."

Jet tossed the piece of rosin on the ground. "So you're saying this is my fault."

Lizzie took a step toward him. "No, I'm saying that you're so desperate for the love our mother never gave you that you haven't been thinking clearly."

"Whoa, whoa, whoa. *What?*"

"I know I'm right, Jet. I've watched you over the years. You throw yourself into anything and everything as if trying to prove something. I've always wondered, but now I think I know why. You're trying to prove your worth. Jasmine left you and you're feeling it again, feeling worthless. As if there's something wrong with you because yet another woman has left you high and dry."

He told himself to ignore the fact that she echoed nearly the exact words he'd said to himself not too long ago.

"Whatever," Jet said, shaking his head. "You're completely off the mark." He turned away only to swing right back. "I was a year old when she left. Trust me, I haven't given her a second thought, not until you and the girls decided to start searching for her."

She stepped in front of him. "Not ever, Jet? Not once?" She placed a hand on his arm. "Because I did.

Yeah, I know I was older, but so what? You grew older, too, old enough to understand that someone left you when you were young, someone who was supposed to love you and cuddle you and watch you grow. Thank God we had Peggy because I hate to think what might have happened to you otherwise."

"Are you done?"

"No. I think you've been looking for someone like Jasmine for a while. Except you were looking in all the wrong places."

"Yeah, well, it doesn't matter now."

"It does matter. I thought for sure you'd be quick to get over her, but you aren't. Damned if I'm starting to think you truly loved her. Really truly loved her. And if that's the case, then you need to snap out of it. You're going to hurt yourself if you keep this up and one member of my family hurt riding bulls is enough, thank you very much."

He huffed and shook his head. "I'm not going to get hurt."

She grabbed his hand, and Jet was surprised to realize he'd grabbed his bull rope as if preparing to leave.

"Please," she said softly. "Talk to her. Sort this all out. I don't want to see my brother hurt, too."

He shook his head.

"Too late."

"Mommy, Mommy, horsey."

Jasmine released a cry of frustration as she ran after Brooke. Dear God in heaven, that was all she needed: for her little girl to get run over by a horse and buggy.

"Brooke Marks, you stop right now!" she yelled.

Gwen tried to pull away, too, but not with as much enthusiasm as Brooke had done. It was Brooke who'd caught the horse bug. Brooke who could talk of nothing but the four-legged creatures she'd gotten to ride at the Roughneck Ranch. It had gotten to the point that even Gwen was getting tired of it. Jasmine had been hoping for some peace if she let her youngest daughter pet a horse again, thus the trip to the Fort Worth Stockyards. She'd taken them to the stockyard stables where they'd wandered the aisles and petted horses before heading out to lunch at Billy Bob's. She'd have thought her child would be done with her horsey fix for the day. Clearly not.

"But Mo-om," Brooke said, but she stopped in her tracks. The driver of the carriage shot her a smile filled with amusement. No doubt he was used to such outbursts from children.

"Don't 'But Mom' me, young lady." She felt sorry for Gwen. She was all but dragging her eldest daughter toward Brooke. "Don't you dare go near that carriage. Not without me by your side."

"It's okay," the driver called out. He pulled up to the curb next to where Brooke had stopped. By then Jasmine had caught up to her. "She can pet him."

She couldn't contain her sigh of frustration, but she smiled up at the carriage driver nonetheless. "Thanks."

"Better be careful," a man behind her said. "She'll be asking for a horse next."

Jasmine's heart stopped. It wasn't the coachman who had spoken—it was someone else, someone behind her.

Jet.

As if echoing her thoughts, Brooke turned around, her whole face lighting up just before she cried, "Jet!"

Oh, damn.

"Jet!" Gwen cried, too.

This time when Gwen pulled away, Jasmine let her

go. She didn't turn around. Didn't want to, but she knew she had to.

He was squatting down, his arms wrapped around her girls, and the sight made her want to cry. Of course. When had she ever not wanted to cry when he was around? Damn it. What was it about him that always reduced her to a blubbering mess?

"What are you guys doing down here?" he asked, drawing back and staring into the twins' faces.

"Mommy took us to the stables."

At last he looked up, and Jasmine felt his gaze like the blow of a wrecking ball. And she knew her feelings for him hadn't faded, not one whit. He didn't hold her gaze for long, however, clearly preferring to focus on her girls.

"She took Brooke to the stables," Gwen corrected. "I wanted to each lunch."

"Which we did," Brooke added. They were always doing that, adding to and finishing each other sentences.

"And now we're going to go shopping for our Halloween costumes," Gwen said.

"We're going to be cowgirls."

It was Brooke who'd spoken, her cheeks full of color, the days of her daughter looking wan and ill long behind her. They'd gotten her blood sugar stabilized. With any luck, they wouldn't have to change her treatment plan for years to come. The shots were still an issue, but that would change soon. She hoped.

"Cowgirls," Jet said, meeting her gaze again. He looked tired. And sad as he squatted in the shadow of the brick building. And something else she couldn't quite put a finger on. "What are you going to wear?"

"Cowboy hats," Gwen answered.

"And a red cloth around our neck," said Brooke.

"And pigtails," Gwen added.

"And Mommy said she'd buy us new fancy cowboy boots."

She cleared her throat. "We were about to go do that." She pointed to the tack store behind them.

"Well, I guess I should go with you, then, being a real cowboy and all."

"Jet—"

But he ignored her, especially when Brooke cried, "Goody!" and took Jet's hand, but not before turning back to the carriage horse and saying, "Bye, horsey. We're off to buy cowgirl clothes."

"Bye," the carriage driver said, clearly amused. "Have fun, girls. We'll be here when you get back."

Jet shot her a look of apology from beneath the brim of his cowboy hat as her girls dragged him away. She followed along at a distance, completely ignored by her daughters.

"I want a pink cowboy hat," Gwen said.

"Cowgirls don't wear pink hats," Jet said.

"They don't?"

"Told you," Brooke said, sticking out her tongue as they crossed the street. It had dawned warm for a day so late in October, and when they stepped from the shadow of the buildings, the sun's beams hit her like a slap to the back. The tack store was across the street, and Brooke bounced along, Gwen a bit more sedate, but both were talking a mile a minute.

"I want a pink skirt…"

"Mommy said we could ride stick horses…"

"I don't think a hat looks good on me…"

"Maybe we could trick or treat with a *real* horse, one of yours, Jet."

The last comment had come from Brooke and it was

said as they entered the tack store, a bell signaling their arrival. The scent of leather and tack soap drifted to her as Jet held the door.

"You don't have to do this," she said softly as she passed by him.

"Yes, I do." His smile was sad, the twins running to a display of boots by the front of the door. "I've missed them."

She couldn't breathe.

She'd missed *him.*

"Look at these boots," Brooke said with all the reverence of someone holding a palm full of diamonds. Despite her emotional turmoil, Jasmine almost laughed. They were the most hideous pair of bright purple boots Jasmine had ever seen. It was no wonder they were on the sale table.

"I think those are the wrong size."

What followed was a half hour of Jet leading her daughters around the store, helping them pick out their Halloween ensemble, and though she wanted to hate him for it, though she wanted to be anywhere other than at a tack store shopping with him for her girls, she knew she was kidding herself. She couldn't get enough of him. He looked so Jet-like in his denim shirt and jeans. He wore a pair of boots, dusty, of course, and the same beat-up cowboy hat she remembered from the day at the branding. When it came time to pay, he insisted on footing the bill.

"I expect pictures," he said as he handed the twins their individual bags.

"Can't you come with us?" Brooke asked. "You could bring Tucker."

His eyes met hers. "No, sweetheart. I can't come

with you. And Tucker's too old, but you'll have fun without me."

It broke her heart to see the look of disappointment on her daughter's face. He bent and gave her daughter a hug.

"I miss you," she heard Brooke say.

"I miss you, too," Gwen said when Jet bent and hugged her eldest daughter.

"I know you do," he said, straightening. "But do me a favor. Give me a moment alone with your mother, okay? Go look at the model horses over there." He tipped his head toward a section of the store that the girls had spent a half hour in front of, oohing and aahing at all the pretty Breyer horses.

"Go on," he urged, following them, but at a distance. "I'm not leaving just yet."

That seemed to appease them, and even though she didn't want to be alone with him, she knew she owed him at least that much. The girls wandered off, still in sight, and just as loud as ever, but clearly reluctant to let Jet out of their sight.

"Thank you," she said, wanting, needing, to control the conversation, to keep it impersonal. "I'll text you some photos."

"I'd appreciate that."

The front door jingled as someone else entered. Someone else laughed at the funky purple boots. Gwen cried out in delight at some toy she'd just discovered.

"I've missed you."

"Jet—"

"No, no. Let me say what I have to say."

She owed him that much. He didn't say it, but she knew it was true. She did owe him. He'd been so kind.

"Lizzie tells me I have hang-ups." He lifted his hat

and ran his hands through his hair. "I don't see it, but she says I was trying to make myself feel better about my mom running out on me or something like that. Like I said, I don't see it, but when it comes to Lizzie a lot of the times she's right, so what I want to say is that I'm sorry. I should have never let that marriage proposal thing get out of hand. I should have put the kibosh on it right away, and I didn't, and it was wrong of me."

It felt as though she swallowed a lump of guilt the size of New York as she listened to his speech. Hangups. She was the one who had hang-ups. She was the one staring into the eyes of a man who loved her and who loved her girls and yet she didn't have the courage to grab that love with both hands.

Lily-livered coward.

"I didn't mean to pressure you, and if I did, I'm sorry."

Oh, Jet.

"Take care of yourself, Jazzie. I'm glad I bumped into you."

She watched him walk away, and still she didn't move. He bent and hugged her girls goodbye. She could have moved then, too. She didn't because she'd been telling herself for a month now that she'd get over him. That she'd broken up with him for the girls' sake. That she didn't ever want them to feel the same sense of loss she'd felt over and over again in her short life. She'd been afraid things between her and Jet wouldn't last. But it wasn't her girls she'd been afraid for—it'd been herself. She was the one who'd been scared and that fear had crippled her. It crippled her now.

The question was…could she be brave enough to overcome her fears?

Chapter Twenty-One

It had been tough to see the twins, Jet thought a few days later as he headed toward Roughneck Ranch as the sun was just beginning to set. Tougher still when he knew that tonight he'd see half a dozen little cowboys and cowgirls, all of them dressed for the occasion.

Halloween.

It was a tradition at the Baron ranch. As children they couldn't very well go door to door. There was no neighborhood. No nearby small town. No nothing. So they'd decorated the ranch and the barns and the ag buildings down by the pasture, originally all for the Baron children, but then their neighbors had started to come. What had started out as one or two families had quickly turned into four and then five and then everyone in the area. Savannah, clever entrepreneur that she was, had recognized a promotional opportunity when she saw one. She turned the Peach Pit, the farm store she managed, into a haunted house. Children could walk from the store to his parents' home, or to the barn—Zombie Land as it was being called this year—then to the various buildings they'd decorated, then all the way back down. What had started out as a private party for the family had quickly turned into a tourist attraction thanks to Savannah, one that required all hands on deck.

Oh, well, something to do.

"You ready?" Savannah asked when he called out to her after entering the Peach Pit. The store was partly dark, the produce and pies she sold covered for the day, the smell of autumn in the air thanks to the cinnamon candle that burned on a counter.

"I can tell you right now it's going to be a madhouse tonight. Jacob was supposed to help out, but he's MIA, no idea why. Lizzie offered to fill in but she's about ready to pop. She should be on bed rest given how late she is delivering, but, oh, no. She insists on helping. I have her keeping an eye on the Haunted Forest from the comfort of a chair."

She hadn't turned to face him, but he could tell from the back that she wore a witch's costume. He was half tempted to razz her a bit—she was his sister after all—but she seemed too frazzled for that. "I have your mask right here."

When she turned toward him, he laughed, his first in days. Maybe even weeks.

"What?" she asked, donning a look of innocence.

She'd hung a fake nose off her face, one of those big, huge, hooked affairs with a massive wart on the end complete with hairs.

"Wait, wait," she said. "You have to see it with my hat."

She turned to her desk, placing something that looked like a stuffed animal on her head, but was really a pointed witch's hat with a wig beneath it, and Jet had to admit, she looked pretty spectacular.

"Funny."

"Looks even better when I'm carrying my broom."

"Where is it?"

"Travis has it outside."

He smiled. Her new husband had been directing traffic.

"Okay," she said. "We've got the barn turned into a zombie apocalypse. The kids will love it. The horses, not so much. We had to move them out. They were freaking at the sheets and the tarps we hung up in the aisles, but wait until you see it. It's perfect. Once the sun goes down it'll be like Amityville. Your job is to scare the bejesus out of the big kids. That should be easy given your long face lately, but here's a mask to help you along."

He took the rubber face—some kind of walking-dead face—she handed him.

"Julieta and Dad are manning the house with treats. This year we've added a hay ride back and forth between the Peach Pit and the house. Next year I think we should plant some corn and do a maze out back, but you know how Dad is." She frowned, and Jet almost laughed again because it made her nose bob.

"Anyway, go. Have fun."

Fun. Yeah. Sure. He clutched the mask and turned.

Jasmine stood there.

He blinked, thinking surely he'd imagined her. But, no. She was there, all glorious woman in her off-white sweater and jeans, long, blond hair hanging down past her shoulders. She was just inside the door, Brooke and Gwen flanking her sides, Gwen taking one look at his sister's face and saying, "Mommy, what is *wrong* with that lady?"

"Nothing, honey, it's just a fake nose." But her eyes never left his own, and there was something in them, something that made his breath catch.

"Well, I don't like it," Gwen announced.

Brooke appeared thunderstruck, too. "I don't like it, either."

"Here, I'll take it off," his sister said from behind him. "See. It's me. Savannah, the peach-pie lady."

Brooke's face cleared. So did Gwen's. "Wow," Gwen said. "How'd you do that?"

"Here," Savannah said, moving past him and then taking their hands. "I'll take you outside and show you. I think your mommy and Jet need to talk."

She glanced at Jet, wiggled her eyebrows and smiled. Jet just shook his head because the odds that she was here to do more than enjoy the festivities were slim to nil.

But he could hope.

"I'm sorry to barge in on you like this," Jasmine said when they were alone. "I ran into Travis outside. He told me you were here."

"No," he said, still dazed. "I don't mind."

"Although I don't think he was happy to see me."

His smile faded a bit. "The family thinks I'm trying to kill myself because of you."

Her brows lifted. "Why?"

He shrugged. "I've been hitting the practice pen pretty hard. They think I'm doing it on purpose, maybe hoping I'll get thrown on my head and put out of my misery."

She opened her mouth before shaking her head a little and then looking at the ground. He saw her shoulders pull back as she took a deep breath. "And are you miserable?"

He took a deep breath, too. "I think you know I am."

When she met his gaze he noticed her eyes were doing that thing again, that sparkling thing that gave him hope for some reason, hope that this was more than just a friendly visit to the Roughneck Ranch's Halloween celebration.

"Me, too," she said softly. "Ever since that day at the branding, I've been more miserable than I can remember in years. And then when I saw you..."

At the stockyard, he silently finished for her, although it hadn't been such a coincidence. Lizzie had told him about her plans that weekend. He'd told himself to stay away, but he'd needed to take some broke-mouth heifers to the stockyard, anyway. He'd just used it as an excuse. If he were honest with himself, there'd been half a dozen times when he'd wanted to drop by the office, too. He'd known Lizzie would give him hell if he did that, though, so he hadn't.

"I miss you, Jet." Her face softened. "The girls miss you, too."

His throat didn't seem to be working, not right then.

"When I bumped into you last week, it made me miss you even more."

"Jasmine—"

"No," she said, holding up a hand, her sweet eyes beginning to glisten. "Damn it. I told myself I could do this without crying."

"Don't cry."

He saw her take another deep breath. "I've been such an idiot. I kept telling myself I broke up with you because of the girls, because I didn't want them to get hurt if something happened and we lost you or you left, but all along it was me who didn't want to get hurt."

"I know."

Her eyes widened. "You know?"

He took another step. They were within inches now, and once again his arms seemed to ache he so longed to hold her. "I'd have to have been stupid not to figure that out. You're afraid, fearful it'll happen again, that you'll lose another person you love."

She wiped at her eyes. "I am."

He finally reached for her, finally pulled her into his arms. "You don't have to be afraid anymore, honey."

She was crying now, quietly, but crying nonetheless. "I know that. I keep telling myself that very thing, but it's so hard…"

"It doesn't have to be hard. I can go back to work at Baron Energies. You could keep on being our engineer. Whatever the future brings, we can handle it. Together."

"You promise?"

"I love you, Jazzie." He leaned down and gently tipped her chin up. "Besides, you're due some good luck, and I don't mean to sound bigheaded or anything, but I'm it."

She smiled. He did, too, and he couldn't hold himself back any longer. He had to kiss her, had to show her without words that he meant every word. She kissed him back, only the sound of the door opening causing them to break apart.

"Jet," Savannah said in a voice he didn't recognize. "I hate to break it to you, but I'm going to have to leave."

Jet drew back, completely confused for a moment. "What? Why?"

When he spotted Lizzie standing behind Savannah, hands on her belly, he knew. Chris, her fiancé stood there, too, a nearly comical expression of panic on his face.

"The baby?" he asked.

"Yup." Savannah ushered Brooke and Gwen inside the store. "It's finally on its way. These little angels are going to hand out candy at the store, if that's okay with Jasmine. Jet, we need you up at the house, unless you want to wait with Julieta and Dad at the hospital, but

we're really hoping you'll stay because we need someone from the family here what with all that's going on."

It took him about 2.9 seconds to figure out she was
right. "Just call us when she gets close."

"Thought you might say that."

"Momma," Gwen said. "Lizzie is having a *baby*."

"I know, honey," he heard Jasmine say.

What followed was a half hour of pure chaos as they
found replacements for everyone. Lizzie and Julieta and
his dad took off, Savannah followed, and Jet found himself in the home he grew up in handing out candy to little kids. Savannah kept him updated, and as luck would
have it—or maybe it was unlucky for Lizzie—the baby
took its sweet time making an appearance. The trick-or-
treaters eventually dribbled to a stop and Jet and Jasmine
and two very excited little girls headed to the hospital.

"Where does the baby come from?" Gwen asked,
headlights from oncoming traffic catching her very
wide eyes.

Jet glanced at Jasmine as he drove. "I'll leave that
one to you."

"The stork brings it, honey."

"A stork?" Brooke asked.

"It's a big bird and it drops little babies off at the hospital for their new mommy and daddies."

"Oh," Gwen said, as if that made perfect sense. Jet
nearly laughed. To be honest, nothing could spoil his
mood. Before they'd left, Brock had even handed him
something, a box. His great-grandmother's wedding
ring. Jet had whispered his thanks to the man who might
seem like a hardheaded, stubborn, son of a cuss at times,
but who really loved his kids.

"Finally!" Carly said when he arrived. "I was beginning to think you got abducted by ghosts and goblins."

"Not quite. How is she?"

"I'll let you see for yourself."

His sister held open the door and there she was, Lizzie, Chris sitting by her side. Brock and Julieta flanking either side of the bed, and what looked to be the rest of the family gathered around. But Jet's eyes caught on the baby in Lizzie's arms, one that was swaddled in pink.

"Girl?" he asked.

Lizzie smiled, and in that grin was all the pride of a woman who'd done the impossible—she'd delivered a miracle. "Jet, meet Natalie Adele," she said softly.

"Can I see, Momma?"

It was Brooke who'd spoken. Jet met Lizzie's gaze and motioned to the twins. "Do you mind if they come in?"

"Not at all," she said.

"Is it real?" Gwen asked as she approached the bed.

Everyone laughed. Savannah came in behind them, Jet having not even realized she'd been gone. She went right to her husband's side, holding his hand as they both stared at Lizzie from the foot of the bed. They were all there now. Carly and Luke, Jacob and Daniel and little Alex. His whole family. It was a perfect moment, one that could only be made more perfect by one thing.

"I have something for you," he whispered to Jasmine, motioning with his eyes that they should go outside. Only when the door to Lizzie's room closed behind him did he say, "My dad gave this to me earlier so I could give it to you." He reached into his pocket and pulled out a box.

She knew what it was; he could tell by her gasp.

He shot her a sheepish grin. "It was my great-grandmother's." But before he opened the box, he began to sink down, right there, in the middle of the maternity ward floor.

"I figure why not make this a family tradition—marriage proposals at the hospital." Her look of joy turned to confusion.

"Lizzie and Chris were engaged at this very hospital." He smiled and opened the box. "And so Jasmine Marks, will you and your girls do me the very great honor of marrying me?"

"Yes, Jet. Of course. Yes!"

He slipped the antique filigree ring on her finger, a ring that had been a gift from his grandfather to his wife after the family had settled in Texas. His grandmother used to say the diamond was as big as Texas, and that it always got in her way, but she'd loved it. He could tell Jasmine loved it, too. He stood, pulled her into his arms, but only for a moment because in the next instant they both heard "Mommy?"

They drew apart. Savannah stood there, a wide smile on her face, both girls peering up at them. It was Gwen who'd spoken because she added, "Why are you hugging Jet like that, Mommy? Did the stork bring you a baby, too?"

Jet thought he heard Savannah choke back a laugh.

"No, baby. Something better. How would you like to have Jet for a daddy?"

Gwen's mouth dropped open. "For reals this time?"

"For reals?" Brooke added.

"For reals," Jet echoed.

The two girls looked at each other, and any doubt that he'd be welcomed by the family was dispelled when they both gave out a whoop and a "Hooray!"

"I knew this was coming," Savannah said, coming forward and giving them a hug.

When Jet glanced down at Jasmine, she had tears in her eyes. His lips found hers without thought, and when she kissed him back he knew she understood what he was trying to say without words. It wasn't a kiss of passion or heated desire, nor of apology and forgiveness, although there was that, too. It was a kiss of patience and understanding, of kindness and love, but most of all, it was the kiss of two people who would be there for each other.

Forever.

* * * * *

COMING NEXT MONTH FROM

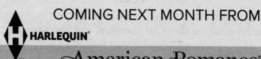

HARLEQUIN®
American Romance®

Available October 7, 2014

#1517 THE COWBOY SEAL
Operation: Family
by Laura Marie Altom

When Navy SEAL Cooper Hansen starts to have feelings for his brother's widow, Millie, he suddenly realizes this might be the most dangerous mission of his military career!

#1518 THE TEXAN'S SURPRISE SON
Texas Rodeo Barons
by Cathy McDavid

Jacob Baron wants to do the right thing for his newly discovered son. But the boy's aunt, Mariana Snow, has her doubts. Can he be the dad his boy needs—and maybe the man Mariana wants?

#1519 HIS FAVORITE COWGIRL
Glades County Cowboys
by Leigh Duncan

Hank Judd can handle his new job as ranch manager and might even survive the arrival of his ten-year-old daughter. Until the woman who broke his heart twelve years ago rides into town....

#1520 A RANCHER'S REDEMPTION
Prosperity, Montana
by Ann Roth

Dani Pettit and rancher Nick Kelly have been friends—*just* friends—for years. But after they share a scorching kiss, Dani can't forget it. Has she ruined their friendship...or discovered she's loved Nick all along?

YOU CAN FIND MORE INFORMATION ON UPCOMING HARLEQUIN® TITLES, FREE EXCERPTS AND MORE AT WWW.HARLEQUIN.COM.

HARCNM0914

REQUEST YOUR FREE BOOKS!
2 FREE NOVELS PLUS 2 FREE GIFTS!

HARLEQUIN®

American ★ Romance®

LOVE, HOME & HAPPINESS

SPECIAL EXCERPT FROM

HARLEQUIN

American Romance

Can't get enough of the **TEXAS RODEO BARONS**
miniseries? Read on for an excerpt from

THE TEXAN'S SURPRISE SON
by Cathy McDavid...

"Excuse me, Jacob Baron?"

Jacob turned. The woman looked vaguely familiar, though he couldn't recall where he'd seen her before.

"Yes."

She started toward him, managing to cover the uneven ground gracefully despite her absurdly high heels that had no business being at a rodeo. "May I speak to you a moment?" Her glance darted briefly to his brothers. "Privately."

"We were just heading home," he said.

"This is important."

After a moment's hesitation he said, "Go on, I'll catch up with you."

"No rush, bro," Jet said, a glimmer in his eyes.

"It seems you know my name." He gave her a careful smile once they were alone. "Mind telling me yours?"

"Mariana Snow."

Jacob felt as if he'd taken a blow from behind. "I'm sorry about your sister. I heard what happened."

Leah Snow. That explained why he'd found this woman familiar. Three years ago he'd dated her sister, though describing their one long weekend together as dating was a stretch. He hadn't seen her since.

HAREXP1014

Still, the rodeo world was a small one, and he'd learned of Leah's unexpected passing after a short and intense battle with breast cancer.

"Thank you for your condolences," Mariana said tightly. "It's been a difficult three months."

"I didn't know Leah had a sister. She never mentioned you."

"I'm not surprised." Mariana reached into her purse. "Leah didn't tell you a lot of things." She extracted a snapshot and handed it to Jacob.

He took the photo, his gaze drawn to the laughing face of a young boy. "I don't understand. Who is this?" He started to return the photo.

Mariana held up her hand. "Keep it."

"Why?"

"That's Cody Snow. Your son."

For a moment, Jacob sat immobile, his mind rebelling. He hadn't been careless. He'd asked, and Leah had sworn she was on birth control pills.

"You're mistaken. I don't have a son."

"Yes, you do. And with my sister gone, you're his one remaining parent."

The photo slipped from Jacob's fingers and landed on the table, the boy's laughing face staring up at him.

Look for
THE TEXAN'S SURPRISE SON
by Cathy McDavid,
*part of the **TEXAS RODEO BARONS** miniseries, in*
October 2014 wherever books and ebooks are sold!